NESI L STONE

Broken Moon Spirit Special Edition

For Kate

Who inspired me to be the wild spirit I am

Also By Nesi L Stone

Broken Moon Spirit
(Standard Edition)

Coming Soon!
Split Between Magic
(Coming Oct 1st 2025)

Trigger Warnings

Abuse
Trauma
Physical Violence
Food sensitivity
Sex

Map

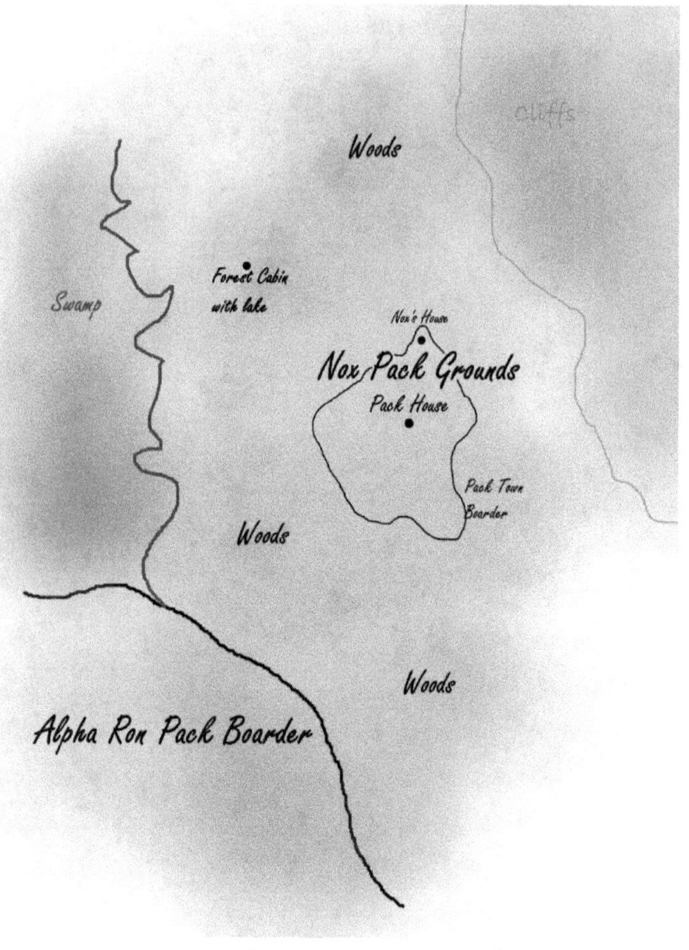

Woods
cliffs
Swamp
Forest Cabin
with lake
Nox's House
Nox Pack Grounds
Pack House
Pack Town
Boarder
Woods
Woods
Alpha Ron Pack Boarder

Playlist

If I don't laugh I'll cry - Frawley
Brother - Kodaline
Home- Machine Gun Kelly, Ambassadors& Bebe Rexha
Better days - Dermot Kennedy
Wings - Macklemore & Ryan Lewis
I'm Good (Blue) - David Guetta & Bebe Rexha
Hazel Eyes - Sabrina Jorden
History of men - Maisie Peters

I

Broken

Prologue

Drip. Drip. Drip. The milky white tears ran down the woman's face, hitting the night sky at her feet. Distorting the stars around her. The small droplets of water sank through the sky and landed on the roof of the building far below. It ran down the side of the building. Weaving its way through the earth, through cracks, around rocks and down deeper than the woman's eyes could see. The little drop darted into a crack in the wall that it had followed into the depths of the earth.

Wiggling through the crack. The droplet slid out of the crack running down the wall and jumping from the wall to land with a small plink as it hit rusted metal.

"I'm so sorry child," The woman whispered.

Nox

"I think it will work out better if we move your border south a mile and I give you the eastern marshes."

"I don't know…I will have to discuss it with my second and Luna," the Alpha of the Blue Moon Pack, Ron, mused. *Oh come on you know it's a good deal. Stop posturing!*

" You can stay here while I think about it," Ron said, waving me off as he rifled through some papers on his desk. "As I am sure you have heard I am looking for my mate, may I continue that here?" I asked, leaning on the door frame.

"Of course." Ron didn't even look up. *What a slime bag.* James was waiting outside the office glaring down Ron's second. "James," I said walking past him, James fell in behind me with one last glare. "Sooo…?" James pondered out loud not looking at me.

"He is thinking," the distaste evident in my voice. As we walked through the halls of the main house the prying eyes of unmated females peered at me from open doorways, and giggles followed behind me. Being an unmated Alpha I was used to the watchful eyes, each waiting to see if they have a chance at the job. None of them were my mate though, so they were of no interest to me.

Our conversation drifted to menial tasks as we left the house and started into the woods. I was distracted by batting the branches out of my face when a scent drifted past me, it was not one of the usual scents of the forest. I could not place it.

Mate

Why is she here?

"What is it?" James bounced off my back. "Mate," I snarled.

"Where? You found her scent?" James struggled to keep up with my long strides through the trees. "Yes," I snipped.

Her scent drifted into the ground. *Fuck. Where the fuck did it go? Where is she?* The trees nearby took the brunt of my anger, I tore my way through bark and branches, the shrub on the ground completely flattened.

"Dude," James gripped my shoulders slowly down my rampage.

"It disappeared underground, she's so close," I snarled.

"It's not over yet," James reassured.

"The nerve of that bitch," A voice echoed through the woods nearby. One quick motion to James and we were hidden behind a bush that was spared of my earlier rampage. Two footsteps stomped through the foliage two metres from our positions. *What are they doing out here?*

"Let's see where they came from." James snuck forward, retracing their steps. A large low concrete cube emerged from the leaves. The only gap in the grey wall was a large rusted door. The breeze from under the door wafted tendrils of her scent from under it. There was no quiet way of breaking the lock, the hinges groan was no quieter. *Be damned the rules.*

An abyss waited the other side of the frame, not even the sunbeams pierced the darkness. Crossing the threshold my eyes adjusted quickly to the dark, a keen hunter's eye. The hallway started to plunge downwards into an onyx pit with each step down the metallic tang of blood grew. *What the actual fuck is going on?!*

"That's blood," James commented, pain and worry echoed in his eyes. Taking two steps at a time, jumping down the last four I gave up on stealth. The cells laid out before me were not the usual cell I had seen many times before, solid concrete and much smaller, no ventilation. *This is a hellhole.*

The scent of blood, dirty bodies and waste matter was blinding, it nearly burnt my eyes. Inching forward sniffing at each door gingerly, each door turning up with the same stench and not a hint of my mate. Each metre down the hall we went the worse the grime was. Sludge inch of mud that went to the end of the corridor. Door after door clanged to the ground behind me. I sniffed at the last door, the scent of my mate drifted through the stench of the air. *Oh thank fuck I found her.*

I couldn't move as I stared at the dark slab of metal in between me and my mate. *She's so close and yet.....* My muscles twitched with indecision. "What are you waiting for?" James asked.

"It doesn't seem real, and this don't feel right," I mutter, frowning.

Her door was more rusted than the rest, thick layers of abnormally dark rust cracked as I pulled the door open. She was curled up in a corner, her body barely covered in a brown shirt, thick chains wrapped around her thin pale wrists. *No, not brown, her shirt used to be white.*

Sage

The dull ache in my joints was a welcome relief compared to the sharp sting of the beatings. Which had slowed and come to a halt a while ago based on the angry scabs forming. I could not help thinking it was some plot to break my soul, or maybe the pack had come under suspicion. They needed to hide the blood on their hands for whatever reason. *It won't last long; they will make up for missed time.*

The distant clang of the doors echoed to my ears. *I guess my time is up.* Door after door banged, and soon footsteps were added to the symphony of sound. *Two? That's not normal....* I inched to a corner slowly as the footsteps drew closer and closer trying not to make any noise. I bolted as far as I could. They paused right outside my door. *Well at least now I know they were here for me.*

Before the door could open I retreated in my mind, shutting out the world. The pain after this would be bad enough I didn't need the memories of the glee and pleasure on their face as they beat me. *I am not here. I am not here. I am not here. Don't let them win. Don't let them win.*

Despite the chant I kept up in my head, fear still gripped my body. A tear slid down one cheek and dripped onto my scrap of a shirt. They were silent outside the door. *What were they waiting for?*

The screams of the protesting door grated on my senses. *Did they not have the key? This was all wrong.*

I risked a glance at the forms standing in front of me. Two large shapes stood in the door frame. I could not bring myself to look in the eyes of the large form standing to the left but the lanky form on the right I could look up and down. The lanky one looked at the other and waited. *No... that couldn't mean..*

I tried again to get another look at the other one's face but my eyes stopped at his well muscled shoulders. *Strong build, dominant presence... that stance; an Alpha.*

My blood went cold. If my Alpha was anything to go by this was not good. *I am dead.* If my Alpha invited another Alpha here for entertainment. *I am definitely dead. He probably won't even notice when I die, he'd be to busy raping my dead body.*

The Alpha took a step forward, a step that was as close to gingerly as an Alpha could manage, down right imposing by any other standard. *Don't let him win. Don't let him win. I am not here. I am not here.*

I closed my eyes, squeezing them shut as the Alpha crouched in front of me on his toes, his elbows resting on his knees, hands loosely hanging in front of him. The warmth of his hand reached my skin before his fingers did, the light brush of his skin against my cold forearm was foreign. *I am not here. I am not here. I am not here. I am not here.*

His fingers wrapped around my wrist just above my cuff, a light tug on my wrist and the grinding protest of the chains filled the room. The anger rolling off the Alpha made the air bristle. He let go of my wrist, which hit my leg with a dull smack as I did not have the strength to hold it up. I waited, going ghostly still, to take the full brunt of his anger. I flinched at the cracking and crumbling of the wall, chunks hitting the floor.

I opened my eyes just a crack to see the Alpha pulling a bloodied fist form the wall. *I am next. Next that will be my skull.* Fear gripped me harder, I could not stop my legs from trembling, sending the shackles on my legs into a symphony of hissing. *Please don't hurt me. Please don't hurt me. Please don't hurt me. Please don't hurt me. Please don't hurt me. Please don't hurt me.*

Over the sound of my chains the quiet whisper of the other one -reminding the Alpha of something- bounced off my mind. Resuming his crouched position in front of me the Alpha reached out again, but this time taking the chains in his hand.

The grinding protest of the metal was unbearable and I let out a small squeak pulling away from him. The muscles in his arms only tightened pulling on the metal even more. With one last protest the metal ripped apart. The scream of the metal breaking echoed in my ears, as he proceeded to remove the other three chains as well. My head lolled onto my knees the entire sequence of events too much for me to handle as my vision started to go black my heart pounding my blood into my skull.

"You are safe now," a deep voice echoed dimly through the fog. *Lies.* The rush of the air against my skin was the only warning I got before the wave of dizziness racked my body. I was held to a hard wall of warm muscle. Then everything went quiet as I slipped unconscious, my body unable to fight any longer.

Nox

She is really here. I have her. I held her tightly in my arms. The warmth and weight of her in my arms is the only thing grounding me. I blinked back the sudden glare of the sun as we surfaced again. *That hellhole.* I had questions, many of them, I didn't care what it took to get answers.

She was completely still in my arms, unconscious. I quickened my pace as the light revealed just how much she had suffered through. What had I done to deserve to see her in this much pain knowing I could have been here sooner and spared her. *Fuck. I could have saved her.*

"Don't think like that," James was hot on my tail. We had been friends since childhood, he knew me better than I ever gave him credit for. "She was suffering," I choked out.

"And now you get to help her heal. The Moon Goddess gives us who and when we need it the most, it is not our place to question that," James countered

"You will find your mate soon," I reassured him.

"I can't wait," he said grimly.

We lapsed into silence, the snap of branches under foot punctuated the sound of our heavy breathing. We were nearly clear of the trees when the sound of voices drifted to our ears. Alpha Ron was talking to the two wolves we had seen earlier. "She is gone."

Quickly ducking back into the dense foliage; we waited till they moved on before making our way to our camp -keeping to the darkness of the forest. "I mean this with all due respect, but I'm pretty sure they can track us from her stench, she reeks," James pointed out.

"You see how you smell after two weeks in there and then you can talk," I snapped. Once within sight of our camp, we ducked out from under the branches. The wolves I had patrolling the camp whipped around at our sudden appearance, dropped to all fours ready to shift at the possible danger.

"Alpha," echoed from each mouth accompanied with a nod of the head, as they straightened up.

"And you brought a girl! How fun!" Jake howled as he walked up to us, slapping James on the shoulder and a slight nod to me. As my Third he did not need to bother with the formalities. "Mate," I growled, holding her a little tighter.

Before Jake could open his mouth and dig himself a deeper grave. A shout from across camp informing us of the arrival of Alpha Ron. I looked down at my mate, limp in my arms, her head resting on my chest, and her fingers tangled in the fabric of my shirt.

"James, you go see what he wants," I could not bare to leave her, not when she was like this, not for an instant. *Not for him.*

James

Fucking hell Nox. He is pissed. Alpha Ron stood with his feet spread, his arms crossed over his chest. Two guards either side of him. "I asked for Alpha Nox. Who are you?" He barked. "I am James. The Second. You can tell me whatever you need and I can take care of it." *Slimy rat.* "The answer is yes," the other Alpha huffed.

"Thank you," The hints of a forced grin graced my face. I waited to see if he would say anything more, he just glared at me. I opened up the link to Nox. *"Pack. We need to get out of here. He knows,"* sang from my thoughts to his.

"Already on it," Nox replied in my mind. "I want to speak with Alpha Kereniki," Alpha Ron finally snarled, "he took her, I know it. Give her back."

"I don't know what you are talking about," I stood my ground.

"Search them," he snarled, his men fanning out towards our camp. *Fuck.* "Alpha," I warned him, stepping up to right in front of him, staring him down. *With all the disrespect.* "Alpha Ron," Nox mused sauntering over. He was dressed in new clothes, no sign of his mate anywhere. "James," he gave me a warning glance. I fell in behind him, not breaking my stare.

" Sorry, I was dealing with some business. What can I do for you," Nox rolled up his sleeve mildly, the air of calm. "Give her back," Alpha Ron snarled.

"Who?" Nox asked mildly.

Nox

My mate was safely packed up in a car, the last of my people quickly packing up the rest. "You know who," Ron snarled. Before I could open my mouth Ron went on.

"I have changed my mind. I will keep our borders as they are. If I find you on my land again I will kill you on sight, and if you don't leave her here when you leave. WE. WILL. HAVE. A. PROBLEM!" Ron shouted, waving his men to his side and leaving without a final word.

My car pulled up beside me and I hopped in. Jake pulled us to the head of the pack as we made the long trek home. I pulled my mate across the backseat of the car to my side. James glanced back at me from the passenger seat. The hours passed in silence. Jake kept his mind on the road, James periodically checking in on me. My attention did not stray from my mate's face.

~

"Dude!"

"DUDE!"

"NOX!"

"ALPHA!" James and Jake's voices echoed through my mind through the link. I snapped awake. "What?" I snarled.

"Your mate," James cocked his head down. My mate was struggling against the seat belt. Any annoyance I had been feeling vanished. I gently pulled the straps from around her. She calmed down significantly without them, but the violent shaking concerned me.

Her teeth chattered so hard they threatened to break. I pulled her closer to me. *She needs to be warm.* She practically threw herself off the seat to get away from me. She scrambled to the other foot well, curling her body into the small space. Her eyes never went above my knee. *No.*

Fuck. Yanking my jacket off quickly. I placed it over her shaking shoulders, her slim white fingers curled around the neck of my jacket. She buried her face in it. *Finally she feels safer.* "How much longer?"

"We are five minutes from the pack house," James updated me.

"Mom. Meet my car, with a doctor and some blankets. Please," I flung out the request to my mom down the link, *"Okay."* The car came to a sliding stop on the gravel outside the pack house. My mother waited outside the house with a blanket over her arm, at the sight of the car she made her way to the drivers

side.

"Do you really think that was my driving? I am in the back," I waited until the last minute to expose my mate to the wind. I quickly tucked the blanket around her shoulders. I pulled her from the footwell and lifted her from the car. *She's too light.* The doctor stood behind my mother. "Bring her to the hospital." the doctor had barely glanced at the shivering bundle in my arms.

"Mate." If not for my heightened sense of hearing I would have missed it. I looked down at her wide brown eyes staring at me. "Mate," more conviction in her voice.

"Yes," I breathed barely above a whisper. My heart thundered in my chest and broke apart at her next word.

"Help."

Nox

I placing her delicate form on the crisp white sheets. *She looks so small.* I leaned back to give the doctor enough space to work. I stopped short at the tug on my shirt, her fingers were still laced in the fabric, now with a much stronger grip.

The doctor walked round to the other side of the bed, he waited for my approval before starting. I gave him a curt nod before turning back to her. *Touch her.* My brain screamed at me to take her and run, hiding her away so no one could hurt her or touch her again. Reaching out to calm myself with her touch, my fingers gently brushed against her forehead, locks of her hair wrapping around my finger tips. "You should leave," the doctor suggested.

"Why? What are you going to do?" Ignoring my questions he went on.

"You just found her, right?" rhetorical. *Yes.* "Your mating instincts are going to be a hindrance to her healing right now." *Bullshit. He just wants to take her from me.* Gently clasping her hands in mine I pulled my shirt from her grip. Placing a small kiss to her knuckles I took a step back, every nerve in my body on fire. At the loss of my touch she curled in on herself pulling the bed sheet over her head. *Oh, my poor mate.*

"She's mine," I snarled at the doctor before storming out of the room.

~

What was taking so long. With each passing minute I became more irritable. *She's mine. I should be with her right now.* The doctor strolled out of her room. I had parked myself just outside it in one of the infuriating plastic chairs. *I am smashing this damn thing later.*

"What is it?" I rushed over to him, noting the distressed look on his face. *She's not ok...* "I am going to be frank. I don't know how she is still alive. The psychological stress alone, but coupled with the dehydration and malnutrition and physical abuse," the doctor shook his head. *Still alive, focus on that.* My blood was a flame in my body raging to get out and tear the world apart.

"Come with me. You can see her," She had not moved since I had seen her last. Still a shuddering mass under the sheet. One of her mud stained feet stuck out from under the sheet. I tugged at the edge of the sheet, lifting it slowly revealing her face. Streaks of tears marred her cheeks, cutting paths down the grime.

A gentle tug on her shoulder brought her to my chest, her presents invading every sense. The feel of her on my skin, her scent in the air, and the sound of her heart beat. "Why does she flinch and pull away, but then cuddle up to me?" My heart broke with each shudder of her body.

"She is traumatized. It is only because of your mate bond that you can reach her. Give her time to heal her trauma and she will be able to connect again, it will take time," The small sad smile the doctor gave me was all I needed to know. This was a battle we would be facing for our whole lives. *Our whole lives. Our. Whole. Lives.*

"She needs to eat, nothing harsh, bone broth would be good. Definitely get her in a warm bath and a change of clothes. Take her home. Keep me updated," the doctor nodded at me.

"Home?"

"Yes Alpha. She can go home with you. She will need some ongoing treatment, but right now her psychological state is more pressing. Her wolf is suppressed," *Her wolf was suppressed???* That was not good, a last measure in most cases. Not many people survived after that, let alone get their wolf back. Her bond will be weakened without her wolf. *Another obstacle.*

"Hungry?" I ran soothing circles on her back in slow even motions. Her head shook only the slightest of movements.

"No? Okay. Let's go home," I looped my arms under her knees and around her back, lifting her off the bed and into my arms. Her eyes stayed looking at the floor as I shifted the blankets to cover her up once again. "Home?" her voice was soft and sweet, like a spring breeze. "Yeah," I cooed.

"No! I don't want to go back!" her soft voice laced with panic.

"No. No. Your new home," I cooed.

My route home took me the long way through all the halls and corridors of the main house. Then I bounced from building to building keeping in the heated buildings. The longest outside trek was to my house on the edge of the woods. The door was locked. *Fuck.* I tightened my grip on her before planting my boot on the door. The wood shattered at the hinges and buckled beneath me.

"My door needs fixing," I linked to James. I carried her straight upstairs, down the hall and into the bathroom. I placed her gently in the tub, she stretched out her legs, toes barely brushing the end of the porcelain. I latched the bathroom door before coming to the side of the tub.

I pulled at the sheet still wrapped around my mate, she bit down on the fabric. *Fine.* I flipped the taps on, filling the tub with warm water. I left my hand hanging in the flow of the water to make sure it stayed at an acceptable temperature. Slowly the water level crept up her body. With my other hand I stroked small circles on her wrist. It didn't take long to fill the tub.

As the warmth seeped from the water and into her body she slowly let go of the bed sheet, it drifted to the surface. I fished it off the surface, it slapped to the ground. The water turned darker with every passing second.

I flipped the water back on, and pulled the plug letting the water flow through running back to clear. Lathering up my hands with a gentle oat soap I slowly rubbed the grime from her skin -there was so much muck embedded into her skin. The water started to cool and her shivering returned.

I started to add more warm water to the tub, but it did not help the shuddering. *Fuck.* I stripped to my boxers and slipped in behind her. My legs sneak down the sides of the tub, on either side of my mate. Though it was cramped -I certainly didn't mind.

Tucked between my limbs my mates shaking slowed. Lathering up my hands one more time I ran them through her hair, the long tangled locks of her hair deep brown. If that was due to the dirt or the actual colour of her hair, I would soon find out.

Sliding my hand down her arm -from her elbow to her wrist- I flipped over her hand, placing the bar of soap in her open palm.

"You can clean the rest of you. I can explore the rest of you later. When you want me to." She began to wash off her face.

"I have left a change of clothes for your friend in your spare room," my mother linked. *"Mate,"* I corrected.

"What? NO!" she screamed down the link.

I blocked her out, shutting her unwanted opinion down. I pulled myself from the tub, I quickly wrapped a towel around my body, trying not to dwell on my body's need for her. Taking a breath to wrangle in all my body parts.

I reached out to pull the wet hair from her face. She jerked away from my fingers before they could touch her, her back hit the side of the tub and she slipped under the water. I jerked to pull her to the surface -pulling her to my chest- lifting her out of the water. Every inch of her, now clean, milky white skin flushed pink from the scrubbing.

Before I could get distracted by her body, I spotted the ribs poking out from under her skin. *She is bone thin.*

In fact her skin was marred with scar after scar. It wasn't just the scabbed over wounds she had to heal from but the many she had already closed up. *Hundreds.* I quickly wrapped her in a towel then added a blanket on top, to head off the shaking before it started. I headed down the hall to my room -placing her on the soft sheets of my bed.

I slipped down the hall to the spare room. There was a pair of pants and a shirt on the bed with a sports bra and nondescript opaque underwear. I scoped up the clothes and returned to my room.

Her towel and blanket were discarded on the floor. *Shit.* Panic gripped my throat, my blood race, but it was an overreaction.

She was curled up in my bed, her brown hair fanned out over my pillow. I pulled at the blanket on the bed.

"I have clean clothes for you," I lightly touched her ankle. *Oh my little mate.* She ripped her foot away from my touch scrambling down the bed. Her eyes never roamed higher than my shoulder. She still saw me as nothing more than another Alpha. I held out the clothes to her. She dressed herself slowly, not taking her eyes off me, distrust evident in every stiff movement, but always respectful and submissive. I watched her as she pulled the clothes over her skin.

Once she had pulled the long sleeves over her hands she let out a sigh. It wasn't that long until her frame was racked with shudders again. *Cold or fear?* I could no longer tell, one I could do more about than the other. I pulled some clothes from my closet. I tugged my sweater over her shirt and some sweatpants over her leggings. *She looks good in my clothes.*

I pulled a blanket from the bed and wrapped her in it. I want to know her name, to stop calling her 'her' or 'mate'. Once satisfied that she would not be cold, I turned back to my closet to find clothes for myself.

Once dressed I wandered back to my bed. Right back where she had been, before me my mate was curled up around a pillow; asleep. Settling down beside her in bed I tried not to pull her close. I lasted half an hour before her scent became too much to bare. She was intoxicating, I couldn't risk it any longer. I rolled out of bed.

I started the shower and hopped under the warm stream. With one hand on the wall, I took care of myself to the daydream of her mouth on me. It did not take long at the thought of her.

Once I had finished I flipped the temperature cold.

~

I had slipped back into bed hours ago.   I jolted from my slumber to my mate tumbling from my bed. I lunged to catch her,but she slipped out of my grasp, hitting the floor with her hip. I gently clung to her, not a peep came out of her. I ran my hands through her tangled hair as I listened to her breathing. *Is she ok?*

Her fingers curled around my shirt tugging lightly on it, I leaned in closer. She brought the fabric to her face, breathing in deeply. I reached for her hip, when my fingers were mere millimetres from her skin she flinched wincing. *Mate.*

As time passed she relaxed, and finally let me hold her again. It was another hour before she let me check her hip. A large bruise was forming on her left hip, but nothing was broken and no muscles strained. By lunch time we had migrated to the living room. She sat in the corner of the couch all curled up.

I got up to make some lunch for the two of us. We had skipped breakfast. *Shit.* A small sound came from deep in my mates chest. I paused looking at her, her eyes were full of sadness, tears welled in her large brown eyes.

"Please stay," barely a whisper left her lips. I didn't move an inch. Her voice was enchanting, I could listen to it all day and never tire.

"Ok," I slid back down to my spot on the couch. Slowly I looped my arm around her shoulders letting it rest there, her shoulder bones dangerously sharp. *She's so thin.*

"Lunch?" The frown that graced my mates face was cute.

"Food?" A flare of panic raced across her face. *Scared of food?* "Ok. An easier question. What is your name?" I asked.

"Does it matter?" she mumbled.

"To me it does," I whisper.

"Sage," she offers.

"Beautiful," I whisper.

"You?" she asked.

"Nox." Though short this was the longest conversation we had had. Now I had her name. *Sage.* "Mate," she whispered.

"Yes," I hummed.

"I'm hungry. I'm gonna make some food. Come with me?" I slowly stood up offering her my hand. I waited for her to take it. She didn't, that stung. She stood up by herself, her eyes slowly riding up my body. My heart thundered in my chest at her gaze. It did not escape my notice that her gaze paused at my hips. The fire in my heart burned hot under her gaze.

Her eyes reached my shoulders and stopped, but only a moment. Her eyes continued up my neck, heating up my blood even further. Her eyes reached my eyes, her shining bright brown eyes looked right at me. *Holy Fuck.* In any other reality, I would have taken her here in the kitchen. "Beautiful," I mumbled to myself.

"Will you eat something for me?" I reached out to touch her hair, I paused before my fingers brushed her skin. "I get to pick it," she demanded.

"Ok." I picked her up and set her on the counter. A smile graced her lips as she swung her legs back and forth. I opened up the fridge, Sage looked over the contents of my fridge. "That. What is that?" Sage pointed at the peaches sitting in the fridge.

"The peaches?" I asked pulling them from the fridge. I placed one in her outstretched hand. She contemplated it for a while, her finger running over the skin of the fruit. I took the other peach and bit into it. Sage watched the juice drip from my lips. How is it that everything she does light a fire in my blood. It was hard to keep the wolf in me at bay. Sage followed my lead and bit into the peach, juice splattering all over her face. We ate our peaches in silence. She made it about half way through the peach before stopping.

"Had enough?" She barely ate anything. She nodded looking

down at the peach, I pulled the leftover peach and ate it. Hers tasted so much sweeter. How was her hair so fascinating to me. It was brown, but if you looked closely at the shades it was a mix of chocolaty brown, deep brown and auburn.

One lock of her hair brushed my finger, Sage jerked back from me. She came dangerously close to falling off the counter. I lunged for her waist, as my hand connected with her waist she jerked away from that touch as well. The pain that laced through my chest at her actions was far more than I expected.

I waited for her heartbeat to slow. *Oh my dear mate.* Her eyes were back down to my feet in submission. Slowly I reached out for her wrist taking it in mine, I ignored her flinch and brought her hand to my chest. My heart was hammering below her fingers, her fingers dug a little into my skin. I pulled her back towards the couch, guiding her down to her pile of blankets. I eased into the seat next to her. Sage leaned up against me, her head resting on her chest.

I just stayed still, her scent calming my worries, I slowly drifted to sleep. My mate in my arms, everything was right with the world. *Mate. Sage.*

Sage

The echoing clang of the door reverberated around the room. I could not become any smaller. What was louder the chink of my chains, or the footsteps of the guard? Every second was a different kind of torture, but nothing like what was about to start.

The guard's hand gripped my forearm, his dirty fingernails biting into my skin. I was dragged into the air by my arm, the weight of my body resting on my shoulder. I wiggled my toes, brushing the floor, trying to reach it as my shoulder screamed in pain. The first hit was a shock to my system, but the second one was laced with more pain. Each hit hurt, more and more, as skin and bone broke under his fist. As it went on my vision got blurry. The edges of the world started to go black.

My head lolled, my eyes rolling to the guards face, swimming in my tears, the familiar face of the guard came into clarity. Nox . It was Nox.

"Sage! Sage! Wake up!" My body was jerking back and forth, a pair of burning hands on my shoulders. My eyes snapped open, Nox's face inches from mine, I pulled away. I was damp and sticky, my skin feeling slick. Despite my attempts to get away, Nox pulled me into his arms, crushing me to his chest. I struggled to free myself of his grip. The image of him in the cell still haunted me. His arms loosened from around me, but my head still rested on his chest. The sound of his heart beat pounding in my ear, my heart beat slowed down matching his.

I relaxed, letting all my tight muscles go; closing my eyes. I started to drift off to sleep. The muffled disjointed sounds of words drifted past my muddled brain, in a silky smooth voice that felt like drinking rich chocolate. My brain tipped with dizziness as I was lifted into the air. The sting of the cold air hit my skin, jolting me awake again.

Moments later we were back inside, the warm air making my stomach roll. My brain drifted to blackness as I sank into a soft surface.

~

I woke suddenly, everything was dark. The whirring and beeping coming from my right scraped against my ears. I blinked to clear the fog from my brain, my eyelashes brushed against something. I jerked back, closing my eyes. I threw my hands out to bat away the object in front of me. My hands waved about in the air. *What?* My fingers flew to my face.

"Gentle," Nox crooned softly, catching my wrists in his large hands. He let go of me as I stilled. What had he done to me? *No!* His fingers gently drifted down the side of my face.

"I am going to remove the bandage on your eyes," he whispered before tugging at something on my eyelids. Gradually the pulling sensation on my eyes eased, I held my eyes closed for a moment longer. I snapped them open once he had pulled his fingers away from my face. I was blinded by a stark white light.

A sharp hiss left my lips as I blinked back tears, once again my hands covered my face. "Turn off the lights." Nox roared. A click not a moment later and the lights dropped dim. A few sunbeams spattered the space from high above windows.

Nox hovered by my side, caught somewhere between sitting and standing. Spots danced in my vision, reaching out for him. I pulled at his shirt. The smile that spread across his face was stunning, it made him look ten times hotter. *What? No.* I can't think like that about him, I don't know him.

An unknown man walks over to the foot of my bed. Panic flared in me. *Who?* Nox paid him no notice. The man flipped through some papers and tinkered with the machines by my bed.

"Alright. Just a couple questions. Ok?" he smiled at me, it was warm enough, but even the worst of my guards could fake a warm smile. I do not trust it. Nox nodded at the man before turning to look at me. His warm smile I trusted. *No, don't trust him. Everyone will hurt you. Don't let them hurt you. Do not let them win.* "How do you feel?" I stared at him watching his every move.

"Sage?" Nox brushed a finger over my face, I jerked to face him, blinking at his face. No, I would not answer. *Don't give them anything they could use.* "Do you remember what happened?" The doctor moved on when I did not answer. *Yes.* Nox was in my cell. I shook my head scooting down the bed away from him, bringing my knees to my chest.

The doctor took a step towards me. *No. He is too close.* "You had a panic attack. I am going to check your eyes." The doctor pulled a long thin tube from his pocket. With a click a light appeared at the end of it. He flashed the light in my eyes a couple times. The light brings tears to my eyes and a flinch to my muscles. The infernal machine at my bedside beeped faster and faster and louder and louder.

Stop. Stop. Make it STOP! STOP! I am not here. I am not here.

The world went fuzzy, Nox's shouting barely making it to my ears. Everything was a swirling haze of white; until it started to dim- fading to black. The last thing I heard was the world ending growl that made the ground beneath me shake.

Nox

The small sounds coming from my mate woke me in the early hours of the morning. I gently placed my hand on her shoulder pressing down lightly -she did not calm. With every passing minute that she did not wake I got more panicked. Shaking her whole frame I begged her to wake.

"Sage! Sage! Wake up!" She jerked awake, her eyes snapping open. A scramble away from me. I looped my arm around her before she got out of reach, pulling her to my chest. I wiggled and squirmed and fought against me. Slowly she calmed down, resting against me. She drifted off into oblivion. *"Doctor?"* I linked.

"Alpha," he responded.

"My mate had a nightmare," I answered.

"Bring her in," I lifted my mate from my bed, she didn't even stir. This didn't feel right. She wasn't just asleep. I damn near jogged to the hospital Sage cradled in my arms. The doctor was waiting for me outside the hospital. His white coat was thrown over his pj's. I must have dragged him from bed, part

of me felt sorry, most of me didn't care.

Setting her small frame on the closest bed, fluffing a pillow under her head. "Middle of the night? Really? It's your best timing yet." The jokes were lost on me. "She was panicking and would not calm down. Then she kind of just crashed." A few questions back and forth, and the doctor seemed to have some ideas. As we talked he set up a heart monitor.

" I couldn't wake her from her nightmare." I watched my mate chest rise and fall as she breathed, at least she was still breathing. *She is still here.* The small plastic chair bit into my back, it didn't matter though. To be here with her I'd sit on hot embers. "Ok." The doctor puttered around, giving my mate some injections. I just sat there, useless, holding my mate's limp hand.

~

I had zoned out long ago just watching my mates face. Her face was not pinched with stress or fear, she was peaceful. Despite that her eyes were tape shut she was so beautiful. Sage started to stir, small sounds coming from deep in her chest.

Her hands went right to her face, clawing at her eyes, waving about in front of her. "Gentle," I hissed. Pulling her hands away from her face. "I am going to remove the bandage on your eyes," I started to peel the tape off her eyes, it stuck to her eyelids so I had to be careful not to hurt her. Her cry of pain racked my heart and she once again covered her face with her hands.

36

"Turn off the lights!" I yelled authority laced every syllable, the lights turned off a moment later. Despite that lack of light my mate still seemed dazed. I stood up and bent over her side, her hand reached out for me, connecting with my shirt and gripping it. My heart fluttered, she reached for me. *Please be ok.* I barely noticed the doctor as he walked over. "Alright. Just a couple questions. Ok?" the doctor said, smiling at my mate. I am watching you. *Don't you dare try anything with her.*

"How do you feel?" Sage didn't answer him. She barely spoke to me. She just watched him, not blinking.

"Sage?" Brushing a finger down the side of her face to get her attention. Her head snapped to me and she blinked a couple times, not really looking at me though -more through me. The doctor was not fazed by her lack of answer -he moved on.

"Do you remember what happened?" Again nothing, but then she shook her head. She was uncomfortable, she had curled up in the farthest corner of the bed. The doctor took a step towards her, the heart monitor getting erratic.

"You had a panic attack. I am going to check your eyes," The doctor flashed a light in her eyes, bringing tears to them. *Stop, she doesn't like it!* She flinched with each pass of the light. If he didn't stop soon I would make him stop. Her heart monitor picked up, and kept rising. "What's happening?! Do something?! If you have hurt her, I swear to the Goddess I will fucking end you right here and now! What have you done?! This is unacceptable!" I screamed at him panicking.

"She's fine. It's just another panic attack," he said coldly.

"Fine?!" I snarled. The growl that erupted from my chest reverberated through my bones, echoing off the walls, making the building shake. "Get out!" the doctor yelled. He had gone pale and was looking at the floor in submission. A couple of nurses pulled me by the arms, apologizing, as they escorted me from the room.

In the waiting room, I smashed every piece of furniture, punched a hole in the wall and stomped around. As time passed I calmed down and worry took over. *She has to be ok.* I walked up and down the middle of the room, waiting was not a strength of mine. "You are going to wear a hole in the carpet," Rebecca commented, she had been checking in on me ever since she had dragged me away from my mate.

"Is she ok?" I asked feeling hollow.

"She will be." The doctor came strolling towards. *Dumb fuck.* "What the actual fuck was that?" I snarled. "You don't want your mate seeing that side of you yet. She had a nightmare, she was triggered. Waking her up sent her into overload." I rushed past him and back to Sage's side, my bones ached to be near her.

I reached out to touch her face, my fingers hovered a centimetre from her cheek. My fingertips brushed her skin ever so lightly, her head leaned into my fingers. She was warm. *Finally.* "How is she?" Rebecca stood at my shoulder looking down at her face.

"She's warm," I gently placed my palm to her cheek, soaking in the warmth.

"That's great," she commented.

"Honey!" a familiar voice called. *My mother.* "Mom," I gave her a tight hug. "What brings you here?" She demanded, her voice stark compared to the quiet. I raised a finger to my lips in warning. "Nox! I am not a child!" she yelped. "Mom!" I yelled back. "What's going on?" she had at least lowered her voice. "My mate had a panic attack," I conceded.

"Right. Your mate," disdain laced my mothers words. "What is that supposed to mean?" I snarled. *What is this bullshit?*

"She is weak. She is no Luna. You are going to reject her," *What the fuck!* I had waited too long to find her, and had not taken another Luna, she will be my Luna. "No. She will be my Luna." I stood up, barring my mom from looking at my mate. She sidestepped me trying to look at her. "Why did she end up in the hospital?" The small pale frame of my mate rose and fell as she breathed. *Still breathing.* I did not answer, if my mother thought she was unsuitable now, after knowing the truth it would be one hundred times worse. "Well?" she prompted.

"Her wolf is suppressed," I sighed.

"She will not be Luna," my mother snarled as she stormed out. The growl building in my chest rumbled, I turned to look at my fragile mate, taking her hand in mine. Closing my eyes. "Your mother?" Rebecca was fussing over my mate's heart monitor. "Yes," I hummed.

"What did she do now?" How that man managed to sneak up on my still was a marvel. "Father," I greeted.

"Wait. Is this your mate?" He stepped up to get a closer look.

"Yeah." Running a hand over my face, I had a day or two's worth of stubble itching my skin. Had I really been here that long? "Let me guess, she said something about her," I nodded, not taking my eyes off my mate. *Sage.* "What was it?" he asked.

"She said; 'she is no Luna', and asked if I was going to reject her." Letting out a low whistle my father rocked on his heels. "She may not be the type of Luna your mother thinks this pack needs, but I am sure she will be the Luna you need." *Ever to diplomat.*

"When did you last sleep?" he asked.

"I'm not sure," I answer.

"Go to sleep son." My father left me watching her, I could not sleep not while she was here. "Nox?" Sage's small voice broke my trance. "Yes?" A broad smile blooming on my face. "Nox." A small smile graced her features. *Beautiful.* "I'm tired," she mumbled and rubbed at her eyes with the back of her hands. "Would you like to sleep with me? I am tired too," I hopped up on the bed patting my chest offering it as a pillow. "Okay." She settled down next to me, not resting her head on me. I will earn her trust. *She is here.* It took some time but I settled into a light sleep

~

I finally had Sage home after another two days at the hospital. She was back to her normal self, well what I knew to be her normal at least. I could not put off talking to my parents any longer. "Mother. Father." I acknowledged.

I was sitting in my office, with them seated on the other side, elbows resting on the arms and fingertips touching. "We just want to get to know her," My mother launched right away. I took a deep breath and looked at my father, who shrugged. *"She's my mate,"* He linked. "Sage is…"

"Beautiful name," my mother cooed, interrupting me. "Extremely fragile right now," I finished. "How so?"

"She is traumatized. I pulled her from a hellhole myself," I snarled. "What?" she asked.

"She was abused. I plan to take it to the council once she has healed enough to testify," I state.

"It's too bad that she went through that, but she will never…" she started.

"Alpha!" James burst through the door, a low snarl left my dad as he stood up. I waved my hand at my father and he sat back down. "Yes?" I asked.

"It's Sage." I bolted down the hall before I even knew I had left my chair.

Sage

Nox . Where was he? I wanted Nox. He said he would be back in an hour at most. *What if he doesn't come back. He has left me.* I tried to pull myself from the couch, its pillowy cushions sucking me back down.

A note sat on the glass coffee table, it was folded in half - Nox's name was at the bottom. I flipped the note open, it was addressed to me.

"Sage. I will be home soon. There is fruit for you in the fridge. See you soon. Nox" Its a trick. *What if its a test?* If I eat he will punish me. He is just trying to trick me into punishing me. He is just waiting for the right chance. *Sleep.* That is what I will do. The couch welcomed me into an uneasy sleep, nightmares plagued my dozing mind.

~

I was not in my cell. *Where am I?* It was so bright. I got up and stumbled from room to room, waving out my hands to find a way out. I knocked thing, after thing, over. I need to be quiet, they can't know I am out of my cell. There has to be a door here somewhere! *Please be a door. Please be a door. Please be a door.*

I crashed through a door. Everything went white. *Pain.* I stumbled forward, the ground uneven, one foot in front of the next. The world dimmed, coming back into focus once again. I was under the canopy of large leafy trees. There were wolves milling around, I could smell them. I kept my eyes on the ground, respect was key to making it out alive.

I ran head first into a wall of muscles, bouncing off of it and hitting the ground. I rolled away from them, panting. Panic gripping my chest. *Air. I need air.* I wrapped my arms around my knees. *So many people.* A hand came into my view, flinching from it. *Please don't hurt me. Please don't hurt me. I am not here. I am not here. So many people.*

Everything is so loud and fuzzy, it's all blurry. Were they here to watch the show of my humiliation? All the faces swirled past me. *So many people. I'm not here. I'm not here.* The mix of their voices jumbled around my head. One of them stepped towards me. *I am not here. I am not here.* I closed my eyes, waiting for the first hit to come. It's too much, I can't.....

I am going to die. *This is the end.* Scared, beaten to death for entertainment. A noise barely registered over the din. There it was again. *Nox?* His voice, I heard it. Was he here to witness this too? *It's a trick.* He is here to help them, to join in.

Strong arms wrapped around me, I tried to wiggle out of them. The muscles tightened, not letting go. *Nox.* He was not hurting me. My heart rate started to go down. Arms looped under my legs and back, I was hoisted into the air.

I grabbed onto his shirt, tears sliding down my cheeks. Why is he rescuing me? Maybe he is not, he just wants all the fun to himself. *No. NO!* The wrath of an Alpha in private. *No! I am not here. They can not win. I won't let them win.* Beaten to a pulp, bloody and bruised, swollen beyond recognition.

I sank back down onto the couch as Nox placed me down. Nox pulled me close to his side, his arm around my waist. The door opened and the voices from outside filled the room for a couple seconds before dissipating again.

The sound of two sets of footsteps echoed through the hall. My grip on Nox's shirt tightened as they made their way closer.

"Sage. It's ok," Nox said as he rubbed small circles on my lower back, my breathing slowed, panic laced my brain as my body relaxed. *Soothed by my capture.*

"What's wrong with her?" Is she okay? She is not good for this pack," a voice I did not know snapped from somewhere in the room. I ducked under Nox's arm, hiding from the mean words.

Nox tucked me closer to his side. I could feel him talking more than I could hear him. His tone was low and warning, almost a growl, it vibrated through his ribs. Nox's arms tightened around me.

"Sage. It's ok. You are ok. Nothing is going to hurt you," He soothed. I was pulled out from Nox's side and onto his lap.

Nox

Neither of us is watching the movie I have on the tv, I am transfixed by her. I had convinced my parents to come back another day, when she is having a better day. *I hope better days come.* I don't know what Sage was doing, but she was avoiding the food I was trying to get her to eat with skill. She had eaten one piece of pear, nothing more. *What can I get her to eat?* So far she liked fruit. *Strawberries? Apple? Mango? Vegetables maybe? Carrot? Avocado?*

"Raspberries," I blurted, Sage flinched at the sound. I wrapped my arms around her, breathing in her calming scent. "Would you try some raspberries?" I just wanted her to eat something, anything.

"I have never had them." Sage was staring at the piece of pear in her hand. "Would you like to try them?" I watched her watching the pear. "No. I am good," she said. She placed the pear on the edge of the coffee table and licked the pear juice off her hand. I tried to ignore what the sight of her tongue running over her skin did to me. *What I would do to feel that tongue on me.*

"Would you try some for me?" I looked away from her tongue, taking a deep breath, her scent was not calming in this manner, it lit a fire in me. *Focus on getting her to eat.* Getting her to eat was a constant battle. "Okay," she puffed, I picked her up, I should probably stop and let her start getting places herself, but the weight of her in my arms -pure bliss.

Setting her down on the counter, taking her still sticky hands -I brought them to my face, breathing in her scent. I smiled up at her, my tongue darting out across her skin. Her skin was sweet with pear juice, once I had taken the time to lick every drop of juice off her skin, I placed a kiss on her palms. I looked up at my mate, her eyes were half closed, a smile on her lips. The closest thing to lust I had seen from her.

I pulled open the fridge door, letting the cool air roll over my skin. I could not get that look out of my mind. I pulled the box of raspberries from amongst the jungle that had become my fridge since Sage mainly ate that. The doctor had advised Sage to start exercising more, as she gained more weight. I guess another reason to stop carrying her around anymore. *I was going to miss that.*

Placing the clean berries in a bowl, I slid it down the counter to her. I dried my hands off and leant against the counter watching her look at the fruit. I picked a couple berries from the bowl, popping them in my mouth.

She watched me eat, before she put one small berry in her mouth. She sucked gently on the fruit. *Fuck.* The Goddess was tempting me today. A smile spread across her face, okay maybe this torture was worth it, that smile was worth everything. She ate one and then another one and another. She finished off half the bowl, the most she had eaten in one sitting so far. She likes them.

"You can have raspberries whenever you like. You can eat anything in the house any time you like." I stroked her hair, the raspberry juice stained her mouth. Oh how I wanted to lick that juice off her skin. "No," she said sharply.

"Why?" I asked.

"It's not mine," she answered, something dark in her eyes.

"Yes it is. This house is yours, everything in it. We share everything." I whispered into her hair. "Please, I need you to eat. For me?" She remained silent for a long time.

"But it hurts." *What?*

"How so?" I asked softly.

"My stomach," she said looking down at her stomach.

"Let's see the doctor. He can make you feel better." I wrapped my arms around her, lifting her up. "I don't want to waste it," she mumbled. Tears rolled down her cheeks. I stopped. "It's not a waste," I whispered as I leaned down, and kissed each fat droplet of water from her face. "It doesn't hurt that much, can we see the doctor later?" she asked.

"Yes." I set her back down on the counter.

"More?" I asked, holding up the bowl.

"No. You eat the rest?" she refused but looked at the bowl.

"Ok." I lifted the bowl, tilted it back and finished off the berries in one mouthfull. Sage watched with a little awe on her face, I smiled at her. She smiled back. *It's almost normal.* If this is the new normal I would be happy. Her smile. It was everything.

"Dude!" James smashed through the front door and stormed down the hall. The smile dropped from her face. Sage scrambled back curling in on herself. *How did she curl up so small?* He had another thing coming. "What?" The rumble of a growl rolling down my spine. I wrapped my arms around my petrified mate. "Oh. Sorry," James looked a little sheepish at the state he had put my mate in. "It's fine," I huffed, letting out a deep breath.

"You are needed at the Council," James informed me as he snacked on the pear that was left on the counter. *The Council.* Though each Alpha governed their own pack, the Council governed the laws between the packs. We could not start wars without reason, so on and so forth. A Council of Elders kept the balance, overseeing the laws of the Goddess. "Why?"

"It's about Alpha Ron," James said as he glanced at the quivering ball in my arms. The one thing that could pull me away from her. If it was anything else.

"She does not leave the pack," I hissed, tightening my grip on her. If I wasn't here to keep her safe, at least the pack would. "She doesn't have to. They only requested you," James said as he rubbed his face.

"When do I have to leave by?" I asked.

"Appointment is tomorrow at eight. You should leave by two this afternoon. I will leave you two alone for now. Your car will pick you up," James updated before he left without another word. I picked her up, I needed her right now. I needed every second with her till I left. Sage groaned in protest.

"Just a couple of days," I whisper more to myself than her.

"I don't want to go." Her voice stronger with conviction, she still was barely louder than an average conversation, but for her it was damn near a yell. "You are staying here," I whispered as I placed her on the couch, "but I have to go."

"No," she pouted.

"I'm sorry. I will be back as soon as I can. Who do you want to stay with?" I ran my fingers through her hair. "You," she mumbled.

"Pick someone else," I cooed.

"No one," she grumbled.

"I don't want you to be alone," I whispered.

"Nox," she whispered.

"Sage," I hum.

"I will be fine," she promised.

"I know you will. I will not be. I want someone here with you." I kissed her head, breathing in her smell. "Wait," she requested. Sage leaned back her eyes looking at me, a small smile pulling at her face. Leaning forward she brushed her nose along my jaw, sparks igniting under her touch. Her lips brushed my cheek, I melted under her touch. A knock rang out through the house, it was James. *Time flies.* "I will be back in three days," I promised.

"I will miss you," she mumbled. *She's gonna miss me?* My heart thundered in my chest. How could I leave now? "I will miss you too," I echoed. I placed a kiss on her forehead. "Fin," I snapped at a nearby guard.

"Alpha," he greeted.

"You are dismissed from your post. You will be guarding my mate," I tried not to snarl and snap. It wasn't his fault I could not stay with her. "Yes," responded. He walked off towards my house. At least she will be safe. I stopped by my office, grabbing some paperwork off my desk. As James and I made our way to the car, we ran into Jake. "Pack is all yours." I clapped him on the back as I walked by.

"Yes sir." He gave me a mock salute. He grinned like a jackal as we walked away. "I want it in one piece," I warn.

"No promises!" he shouted back.

"Please try to keep on the paperwork!" My office door slammed shut behind Jake.

Sage

He is gone. My…Nox .. is gone. It was odd to miss him, but I did. Why did he go? Was this a game? To hurt me? He left other people here. I hugged my knees to my chest, rocking back and forth. My back knocking into the wall with a small thud and a lace of pain up my spine. What are they going to do to me? *Don't let them win. I am not here.*

"Do you want some food?" It was a test. If I took the food he would punish me. He placed a hand on my shoulder. I locked up my muscles, and did not react. It would only make things worse. They want the reaction. *Do not let them win.* I stay put on the couch. The only indication of time was the sun setting. They did not leave, the two males stayed all day. Moving about the place. They did not relax in their vigilance, nor did I.

The plate of mixed fruit they had placed on the table hours ago still sat there, the raspberry on the top tempting me. "Sage. You need to eat." The male tried to give me the plate. I kept my eyes lowered to the floor, not giving into them. One of the males stood in front of me rolling up his sleeves.

"I talked to Nox about your sleep schedule," he informed. He talked to Nox? He was in on this? *Nox.* The male wrapped his arm around me. I curled up in myself even tighter, being in a ball made it harder to move.

Despite his groaning, he did a fairly good job moving me. He didn't drop me. He kicked the door open, nearly toppling over. He walked into Nox's room. *Our.* When did I start thinking like that?

He dropped me on the bed, in the middle. I bounced a little, before settling on the thick blankets. Nox's scent swirled around the door. *Calming.* The male shifted uncomfortably, he didn't like being in Nox's space. I mean he was in his Alpha's personal space, whether or not it was permitted.

"Goodnight Luna." He left as quickly as he could. Once he was on the other side of the door he stopped, and stood there. I buried myself in the covers of his bed. *Safe.* I wish he was here. It was warm here. Here is good. *Nox.* My muscles started to ease, and relax, my breathing slowing, my thoughts slowing.

A sound. What was that? I rocketed right back to high alert. I curled up under the blankets, going still. Listening. There it was again. It was the floorboards creaking under the boots of the male outside.

It took some time to relax, but with Nox's scent all around me I slowly started to. I was too jumpy. I didn't realize how much Nox did for me, to me. He calmed me down with just a touch. I couldn't stay here. *Where was Nox? I need to find him.*

I paced back and forth across the floorboards, avoiding all the loose and creaky ones. I need to stay under the guard's radar. My eyes darted to the dark corners and windows. I walked over to the large walk in closet, I ran my fingers over all the clothes hanging in there. All Nox's, none of mine. I mean I have never had clothes to hang, let alone a place to hang them.

Maybe that would change. *Stop thinking like that.* I tugged one of the large black sweaters off its hanger. Pulling it over my head, Nox's scent mingled with mine. I liked that scent almost better than Nox's, *almost.*

I stopped before the door, waiting, wringing the cuff of the sweater. I took a deep breath. Wrapping my hand around the cool metal of the door. I twisted the handle slowly, pulling the door open only enough to let a sliver of light through. I waited, nothing happened. I pulled the door open, a broad set of shoulders greeted me. The guard was still at the door. He turned around quickly, I slammed the door shut in his face before he could make a sound.

I ran back to the bed, the boards creaking under my bare feet. I flung the blankets aside, flopping onto the mattress pulling the blankets back over top of me. My breath heated up the space under the blanket.

It took longer to calm my heart and breathing, even with Nox, *delicious,* scent filling my head. I need to get out, away from these other males, and get to Nox. He was my mate. He would not want me near other males. Mated males were overprotective of their mates, especially Alpha's.

The window. I could go out the window. I peeked out of the window, the night was dark, but the sky was starting to lighten along the horizon. The drop from the window was long but not unmanageable. I gently pressed on the cool glass, swinging the window pane open.

I shimmied onto the window sill, I gently lowered my body to hang from my arms before letting go and dropping to the wet lawn. I wiggled my toes as the mud slipped under me. It was wet and cold.

I ran into the trees, dodging roots and rocks that stuck out from ground, ducking under low hanging branches. I ran and ran, my legs burning. *Nox.* I took one more step and my legs buckled under me, unable to go farther. My body hit the mossy ground with a squelching thud. I rolled onto my back, the moon light hitting my face from between the trees.

A small twig snapped from under a bush beside me. I sat up, my muscles protesting, a small rabbit hopped out from under the leaves. It was small and round, all black fur, it was cute. *So cute.* I rolled onto my stomach, the mud seeping through my clothes. I reached out my hand, palm down, sliding it through the mud towards the small animal. Its nose twitched, once, twice, its head whipped around to face me. It went still.

Its only movement was its nose -twitching. I watched, not moving, as it calmed down. *Was this how Nox thought of me?* It slowly returned to its rabbit-y ways. Its nose twitched as it investigated the grass. As it worked its way slowly towards me, I watched, its small paws taking small step after step.

It was barely a foot from me when it looked right at me, still silent, watching. Its nose twitched smelling me. I smiled watching its shiny eyes. *Theo.* The little rabbit would be Theo. I wiggled my fingers towards Theo. He stilled, twitching, I stretched my arm out a little bit more. I could almost touch him. I stilled, waiting, Theo's nose twitched. He lifted a small fur covered paw, he reached out, placing his cold wet paw on my hand.

I rolled over scooping his small frame up in my hands. I felt his warm body resting on my shoulder, a small weight. His heartbeat was wild on my skin, beating right out of his chest. I waited, not moving, and it started to slow.

I had not made it very far from the house, barely near the pack border. The guards would find me quickly, I could not outrun them. Maybe I could get back and they would not notice I was gone. At least there, Nox would know where to find me. Even if there were other males there.

I climbed up the outside of the house and back in the window I had left open. Crawling back under the covers of the bed, I placed Theo next to me. He wiggled about the sheets for a while before settling down in the warmth.

The sun rose fully into the sky, warming the outside world. The guard at the bedroom door knocked, and then slowly opened the door. His eyes on the floor. *Respect for me? But I was no one.*

"How are you Luna?" he asked quietly from the door.

"Fine," I forced out as loudly as I could. He left after that, closing the door behind him. I waited not letting my smile spread on my face. I pulled back the blanket Theo's small body sleeping beside me. His small chest rising and falling. I smiled.

I curled up around his small form, letting sleep take over me.

Nox

I had made good time with the council. I had been able to leave several hours early. I speed down the roads, ignoring the speed limits. I had been getting updates from Fin throughout my time away. After the first day Sage had refused to leave our bedroom. *Was she nesting?* That was wolf behaviour, hers was repressed. *Maybe her wolf was coming back?* Either way, she was not eating enough and I needed to get back to her.

I ached with need for her, in more than one way. "Careful. There are speed limits," James drawled, as I raced down road after road. I just wanted to be near her.

"I know you want to get back as fast as you can but if you crash you may never see her again." *Asshole.* Asshole though he was, he was right. I slowed -a fraction. After several hours, the familiar highway that led to my pack was disappearing under my wheels. *Soon. I will see her soon.*

"Stop thinking with your dick," James snarled as I sped up even more. I growled at him. *He was keeping me from her.* "Stop being a dick, it's a wonder she spends any time with you," He linked, ignoring my warning.

"Dude get it back in your pants. She is still the same fragile wolf as before. I don't want you scaring her off." *Fuck. He was right. Asshole but right once again.* "Fuck you." I linked back. An absolutely wicked smile laced my seconds lips. He was my second for a reason, he knew when to shut up and when to put me in my place.

"Hold on," I matched his wicked smile. I pulled down the small gravel road to the pack. My foot hit the floor, the car jolted forward. Skidding through the pack house parking lot, and down towards my house.

Skidding to a halt in my driveway I threw the door open and leapt out. I left the car door open, taking the steps to my new front door two at a time. I nodded at River who stood beside the door. He pulled it open for me. "Alpha."

"Alpha," Fin greeted me as I strolled through the door into the main room. He stood on guard. *What was wrong? Is she okay? Why did he not say she was ok in his reports?* Panic gripped my chest. "What's wrong?"

"Nothing," I relaxed a little, as he saw me relax, so did he. He.. oh right I am the Alpha of this pack. I did leave him to care for my mate, his Luna, in my personal house. Not a comfortable task for any wolf. If I am being honest Sage is not the easiest to care for either *-but she was so worth it.* "Luna's in your bedroom," He reported as I moved through the house. Though she had not been sworn in yet, she was their Luna. That was half the battle she faced, the approval of the pack. Despite what my mother thought she was doing great so far.

I smiled at Fin, before darting up the stairs. A thundering mass -as I practically jumped up on them. I stopped outside my bedroom door. *Our.* I leaned against the wooden door frame. Waiting for my body to slow down, if I went in there as a thundering mass of energy she would not be ok.

As slowly as I could muster I opened the door. Sage was curled up in the middle of the bed. Though she had not been nesting in the technical sense, it still felt the same. Her scent was all around the room, blankets and clothing built up on the bed.

I smiled at the relaxed nature of her body, though she was curled up it was loose -her muscles did not hold their usual tension. The urge to curl up with her and waste away all of time gripped me. I made my way to the bed, I knelt on the edge of the mattress. I leaned over, reaching out an arm to support my weight.

Her hand snapped out and caught my wrist before it reached the bed. I leaned back to avoid smashing into her. Her large brown eyes looked up at me. "What is beautiful?" I reached out my finger tips running down the side of her face. A small smile gracing her face -oh that smile- I had missed this. *Her smile.* She fidgeted nervously, not looking at me.

"It's ok." She seemed better, despite the evidence that she had not left this room and had barely eaten. She was more open and communicative. I tucked her hair behind her ear, I wanted to see her face. Sage slowly lifted the blanket off her legs, oh those beautiful legs. Tucked between her bare legs was a small rabbit. She brushed a finger over the rabbits head. It seemed content.

"I want to keep him," she whispered. Sage wanted to keep this small animal? *Fuck.* How could I say no. "Okay," I reached out and ran a finger over the rabbit's fur. "Can we get a doctor to check him out?" I asked.

"Ok." I held out my hand, Sage placed the small creature in my hand. "Hop on," I offered. I bent down offering my back to her. Sage climbed up on my back, she was warm from the bed, her scent was mixed with mine. *Oh holy hell. Intoxicating.* I waited trying to get myself under control. "Nox," she whispered.

"Yes?" I breathed.

"You smell good," Sage commented.

"What do I smell like?" I asked.

"Safe. Happy," she breathed.

"Theo," She said, as she reached out a hand to me.

"Who?" Another wolf's name from her lips, after she was away from me so long.

"Rabbit." Oh, right the rabbit.

"Here." I placed the small black lump in her hands. She placed the rabbit on my shoulder, its small claws digging into my skin. *"Doc? I realized this is an odd request. Can you check if a rabbit is healthy?"* I linked the doctor as we walked down to the hospital. "Doctor!" I banged through the hospital doors.

"Yes." One of the several medical students strolled out of the doctors office. "Alpha," he greeted -wide eyed. "Your lucky day! How much do you know about rabbits?"

" A little," he answered.

"Good."

"Just make sure Theo is healthy," I commanded. I handed the poor student the rabbit and walked away. I knocked lightly on the door of the doctor's office, before opening it and walking right in. "Alpha." He didn't even look up from his paperwork. I bent down to let Sage off my back, but she just held on tighter. Though I delight in her touch, I needed the doctor to be able to see her.

"Sage hasn't been eating enough as of late," I reported. I tightened my grip on her knees. Though my beautiful mate appeared to be resting -her head on my shoulder eyes closed- her muscles were stiff. "May I ?" He stood up. I nodded, holding still so he could come look at Sage with the least disturbance.

"The doctor is just gonna check if you are ok," I whispered to her. Her eyes opened and she blinked a couple times. Sage nodded looking up at me. I missed her voice. Sage pulled away from the doctor as he came closer.

I steeled myself, I could not retaliate, even if every small flinch enraged me. Once the doctor was done poking and prodding I pulled her from my back to my arms. I eased into a chair, resting her on my lap. I stroked her hair, more to sooth me than her. "She is losing weight again," he stated.

"Sage. You need to eat more. It's important," he instructed her. I didn't like his tone. It was patronizing. A growl, low and warning escaped my lips, rumbling through my ribs. Sage slipped from my lap to the floor. Wrapping her arms around her knees. I pulled the chair away from her, sliding down beside her, my legs either side of her.

I pulled her close to me, I pulled her hair out from under her arms where it was caught I tucked her hair out from her face. It was splotchy and pink, tears dripping from her cheeks. I rubbed her back in slow circles, the grip on her knees loosen.

"Nox." She wrapped her arms around my neck pulling herself onto my lap. Her legs wrapped around my waist, her weight resting on my hips. *Oh Goddess, give me self control.* I closed my eyes, running my nose along her neck. One day -soon- I hoped it would sport my mark.

Tears dropped onto my shirt, I kissed her forehead, my fingers skimming over her silky locks. I hooked my arms around her waist, standing up. I walked out of the office without another word. "Alpha." I paused at the door.

"I'm sorry, but her health is in danger. She needs to eat more. Not just fruit." I nodded as the doctor went back to his paperwork. The med student was squatting down to look into the rabbits eyes. I picked up the rabbit, placing it in Sage's hands. I walked quickly to my house, taking the distance with long strides.

Now that I was back, all the guards I had milling around while I was gone had returned to their posts. Skipping past room after room, I bring her to our room. Placing her on our bed, she was curled up in a ball, around Theo. I pulled a couple of blankets over to her, wrapping them around her. I hated that the rabbit was giving her more comfort than me. Her mate. *If she could even understand the bond.*

"Don't go," she whined from behind me. I had turned to let her rest. I turned back to her, she had crawled out of her blanket cocoon, and to the edge of the bed. Her big bright eyes watched me. I came over and sat down next to her. She placed Theo down on her other side, she climbed into my lap. I smiled down at her, I buried my nose on her hair. "I missed you," I hummed. *Would she ever feel the same?*

"I missed you too." Joy bloomed in me.

Unknown

I had to find her. The mossy forest flies past me.

Sage

I rolled over in bed, it was cold. I reached out a hand, looking for Nox. He wasn't there. *Nox.* I ducked under the covers, breathing in Nox's scent. I tucked my knees to my chest. The creak of the door filled the room, footsteps followed. If I didn't move they would not notice me.

A hand grabbed my foot, it was outside the blanket.I tugged it out of their grip back under the covers. The covers were ripped from me, cold air flooding my skin. Nox looked down at me smiling, I smiled back at him. I stretched out my arms towards him, he lifted me up, and wrapped my legs around his muscled torso.

Nox sat me down on a chair in the kitchen. I looked at the variety of food in front of me. Waffles, pancakes, bacon, yoghurt, fruit, toast, and about 7 different jars of jam. I stared at the large amount of food. *It was all too much.*

Nox placed a plate in front of me, placing a waffle on it, then a slice of bacon. A dollop of yoghurt on the side, then fruit piled on top of it. I looked at Nox. Did he think I would eat all that? "Please," I answered, he was waving about maple syrup.

"One bite of each thing, then eat as much of whatever you like," he instructed. I stabbed the waffle with my fork. I could do one bite. I slowly chewed the sticky sweet waffle. It was amazing, I took another bite of it. I scooped up some of the yoghurt, trying that. I didn't like that as much, it was thick and gummed up my mouth.

I picked up the slice of bacon, biting down on it. It was salty, it was amazing, but as the salt faded it was gross, greasy. I spat it out on the counter glaring at it. Nox was laughing. I hugged my legs, he was making fun of me. "I'm sorry." He stopped laughing, his tone serious. "I'm not laughing at you." His hand rested on my back. "I don't like bacon," I comment.

"Ok. You don't have to eat it," he said. His hand ran small circles on my back. I swiveled in the chair to face him, wrapping my arms around him. His head nuzzled into my hair, he liked my hair, he was constantly touching it. "I'm glad you found me," I whispered.

"Me too," he mumbled. Nox's nose ran down the side of my neck. I breathed in this scent, his breath fanned out over my skin. A small rumble deep from Nox's chest, I leaned my head back. Nox's lips gently traced the same path his nose had just.

My heart hammered, it felt so good. *Mate.* Something deep within me woke at the rumble from Nox's chest, rising to meet him. *Mate.* Nox continued to place small kisses down my neck, continuing down my sternum, stopping a couple inches down. The rumbling in his chest built into a low growl. Unlike all the growls I had heard from him before this one was sensual, and warm -not aggressive.

That growl heated up my blood, flushing my skin. Nox's hands gripped my hips, pulling me flush against his skin. Nox's breathing was heavy, his breath warm on my skin. "Sage," he murmured.

"Nox," I replied. I placed a hand on his chest, his heart thundering under my palm. With my body this close to him I could feel his desire for me pressing into my thigh through his pants. I leaned over and placed a kiss just above my hand. I rocked forward pressing myself against him, another growl from Nox at the contact. I nuzzled my face against his neck, his fingers digging into my skin.

A knock rang out in the space, the growl that came from Nox was not deep and sensual, annoyed at the interruption. Oh the poor soul who interrupted was gonna regret it. Nox walked over to the door not bothering to hide what was going on in his pants.

He came back with a guard, who shifted uncomfortably. Nox did not look happy, the remnants of his lust still hung in his eyes, plainly evident in his body. I had hid behind the counter, crouched on the floor. Peeking out from the corner. The guard stood in the kitchen looking at the floor. Though Nox rarely enforced rank and proper protocol, to see the guard in submission now was understandable. Nox was all power and annoyance.

"Alpha. Luna," the guard greeted stiffly. All the fire and

confidence melting from me, I waited, their hushed conversation not registering in my brain. The guard was pacing distressed, and soon the muscles in Nox's shoulders tightened. I crawled towards the living room, slowly making my way along the floor. I almost made it to the safety of the living room, unnoticed. "Where do you think you are going?" *I froze, oh no. Was I in trouble?* Nox's hands slid over my hips, and lifted me into the air. I was tucked safely in his arms.

"I.. You.." The guard was still in the room. I glanced at him, he was frowning at me. I looked at the ground. "Sage," Nox probed.

"You were worried. I didn't want to get in the way," I mumbled.

"You weren't," I asked, nervously. Nox sounded so confident in his words. "Are you sure?"

"Yes," he answered and smiled at me, I smiled back, wrapping my legs around his waist. I ran a hand over his shoulder, inciting a rumble from Nox. "Thank you for the update," Nox dismissed the guard. "Can we go for a walk?" I asked. The sun was shining brightly outside.

"I wanted to return to where we left off," Nox placed a couple of kisses on my shoulder. His teeth grazed along my skin. "There are rogues in the area. Its not safe. Tomorrow?" He was back to playing with my hair. "Please," I begged.

"Where is Theo?" Nox changed the subject, trying to distract me. I wrinkled my nose at him, huffing. I pointed up the stairs towards our room. "You left him alone in our room?!" Nox stood there, shocked for a moment. He placed me on the floor before darting upstairs. I waited for him to come back. He didn't. I started my way up the stairs after him.

As I walked into the bedroom, Nox was pulling Theo from our bed. *Our bed.* That would never get old. "You left him in our bed?" he snapped. Nox was annoyed with me.

Nox handed me Theo and left. *Where did he go? Was he leaving me? Was he seeking the comfort of another? A female?*

Theo's small warmth and twitching nose could not calm me. My mate had left me here alone. I had made him mad, crossed a line. He was an Alpha, his rage would be devastating. I had been so foolish to let my guard down. *What was I thinking?* This was not my pack, my house or my room. It was all his, I was just the current female warming his bed. *That hurt.*

Nox walked in several hours later. He didn't look mad, that doesn't mean anything, it could be a trick. I sniffed at the air, he did not smell like another female. *He had not sought comfort in another.* He could not see me from his position by the door.

He scanned the room, as time passed his heart beat picked up. He took a couple steps forward. He spotted me curled up by the nightstand. He stomped over towards me. He was still mad. Please don't hurt me. *Please.*

"I'm sorry. Please don't hurt me," I begged. Nox stopped in his tracks. I could not read the look on his face. *Oh no I had said that out loud.* He crouched down, coming to my eye level, he looked into my eyes for a long moment. "I would never hurt you," he insisted. Nox stayed in his crouch, not touching me. He was angry.

"You are mad?" I fidgeted.

"Sage. I am not mad at you. I am worried." *He is not mad?* "You are not mad?" My heart beat slowed. "No," he answered. Nox smiled at me, warmly. I crawled forward reaching out to him. He pulled me into his lap, wrapping my limbs around him. His fingers found their way to my hair, his nose in my neck. I could feel his heartbeat calming under my skin. *He was really worried about me?*

"I got a gift for you. Well it's for Theo," he informed me. I gripped his shirt as his fingers stroked my neck, they sent little sparks down my spine to my hips. "Really?" Nox was warm, and comforting. Nox pulled me to his back, wrapping my legs around his hips, I rested my head on his shoulder blade. "Come. I'll show you," he said, as he picked up Theo and made his way to the back door.

"Outside?" Nox yanked the backdoor open, the muscles in his back flexing under my face. It was delicious, the feeling of his muscles. "Yes." He placed me back on my bare feet. He walked out into the sunlight, I stayed where I was, vaguely remembering Nox's warning of rogues. Nox held out a hand for me, I took a step forward taking his hand. The sunlight hit my skin, I smiled at its warmth. Nox tugged me gently to his chest, wrapping me in his arms. I smiled into his shirt.

"For you," Nox said as he turned me around to face away from the house. There was a cage in front of me. It was taller than me, it was full of coloured tubs and ramps. It looked fun, lots of toys. "But it's for Theo," I said.

"Yes," he hummed as I placed Theo in the cage on the soft wood shavings. I rubbed my nose against Theo's cage. "Do you like it?" Nox asked.

"Yes," I whispered as I wrapped my arms around his neck. A loud crack echoed through the woods beside us. Nox tugged me behind his body, hiding me behind his broad shoulders. He was fixated on the woods. I scanned the woods through the gap in his arm. "There!" I pointed to a pair of beady black eyes hidden between the leaves. The eyes disappeared as Nox found them.

"Inside," Nox snarled. Nox lifted me into the air. My hips slung over his shoulder. Nox slammed the door behind him, locking the door. He gently placed me on the couch. I looked at his eyes, his eyes were glowing yellow eyes. Wolf eyes where his usual eyes were. His pure Alpha eyes staring back at me, I held his gaze. He was scared, threatened.

I placed my hand on the side of his face, not backing down from the raw power rolling off of him. "Mine," his voice -a snarl, barely human, his teeth bared.

"Sage," he growled. His eyes did not blink. "Mate," he hummed. He was hurt, panicking, his life threatened. His wolf was fighting for control, to fight whatever was threatening him.

His canines peeked out from his lips.

"Nox," I whispered. Nox nuzzled into my neck pulling me close to him. His canines grazed over the skin of my neck, running up my neck. As his teeth reached my hairline behind my ear a sharp pain laced my skin momentarily. Every muscle in his body went rigid. His tooth had nicked me, a small bead of blood ran down my neck.

"I'm so sorry," Nox's voice broke, my mate's world shattering before my eyes. *No. I am ok.* "I'm ok," I reassured. Nox's yellow eyes watched me. Slowly he leaned in his nose running up my neck, pausing before the blood on my neck. The slick warmth of his tongue ran up my neck, cleaning off the blood. He placed a gentle kiss on the small cut.

He wrapped me in a blanket, pulling me into his lap. His arms and legs cradled me to his chest. We stayed there all afternoon, his heartbeat and breathing a gentle song to my ears. He stayed on high alert for many hours, his eyes staying yellow the whole time. Not once did I back down from them, he was scared, set back to his basic instincts.

At some point in the afternoon two males came to talk to him. One look at his eyes, and their eyes hit the floor. They tried to ask some questions but all they got was a growl that sent them scampering. What had scared him so much? I could not complain about an afternoon spent cuddling with my mate.

Sage

I laid in bed, watching the shadows on the ceiling. I strained to hear what Nox was talking about downstairs, or even who he was talking to. He snuck downstairs, after he assumed I had fallen asleep, which I had not. I hadn't been able to get the memory of his tongue on my neck out of my head -it had lit a fire in my hips. I ran my fingers down the side of my neck.

I couldn't risk getting any closer, he might catch me spying. I let out a breath, dropping my hand to the bed. This was too much, who was he meeting? Why was I left out? He was my mate. I clawed my way to the edge of the bed through the many blankets that filled our bed. *Our bed.* He shared his bed with me. I needed to trust him. *He needed to trust me.* He was my mate, but our bond was not completed.

I gently placed my feet on the cold floor, slowly I made my way across the floor, avoiding the loose floor boards. I gently pushed on the door, Nox had left it ajar when he left, all I had to do was push lightly on it. I slipped through the small gap.

I paused in the hall, the voices a little louder out here, still not clear. I started down the stairs, slowly pausing on each step.

The light in the kitchen was on, I slipped into the living room across the kitchen. I hid in the shadows behind the couch. The words drifted in from the kitchen clear as day.

There was an unfamiliar man in the kitchen with Nox, both were looking at the multitude of maps spread all over the table. "We still haven't found the wolf. We think he got in here," the unknown man said.

"I want all borders strengthened," Nox added. Both men went quiet in deep contemplation. In the quiet I shifted my weight from one foot to the other. A small sound from outside broke the silence. It went ignored as a sound of the night. Then it dawned on me from where the sound came from. *Theo.* The sound was Theo. *It was Theo!* My grip on my shirt tightened as I tried to calm my breathing.

Nox and the other man were now looking right at my hiding spot. They had heard me, the shadows still concealed me. Both of them crept forward, bent down ready to shift at the first sign of a fight. Something was wrong with Theo and they were hunting me down. *They were hunting me. Nox was hunting me.* Tears dripped down my face, they were hunting me. Nox stood up straight grabbing the other's arm, stopping him in his tracks.

"Sage," Nox whispered. I stretched out a hand towards him. He grabbed my hand pulling me to my feet. I slammed into the wall of muscle that is Nox's chest. He crushed me to his body, I gripped his shirt. He was not hunting me. *I am safe.* The sound from outside repeated. *Theo.* I pulled away from

Nox, tugging on his shirt.

"Theo," I whispered. It took me a couple tries to get his name out loud enough for him to hear. He seemed to understand what I wanted. He lifted me up, wrapping my legs around his waist bringing me to the back door. He set me down as he pulled open the door. He took my hand as he guided me into the cool night air.

I barely paid notice to the other male who followed us. A dark shape was moving around Theo's cage. It was a person. *Theo!*

"Hey!" Nox snapped. The growl that Nox unleashed on the figure was otherworldly. It rippled through the night, power laced through the sound, even I was tempted to submit to him. Through the darkness I could almost make out the face in the dark, he looked up, directly at Nox. He bolted into the night. My eyes zeroed in on what he carried in his hand. He had Theo. I battled against Nox trying to go after him.

"Get the guards on his trail," Nox ordered, to someone -who I did not know. I dropped to the ground slithering from Nox's arms. I didn't even notice when Nox picked me up and carried me inside, but I found myself being tucked up in bed. Nox knelt on the floor in front of me, his hands resting on my knees.

"We are going to get him back," Nox whispered, he wiped the tears from my face. I crawled back under the covers, Nox following right behind me tucking me against him, his arm around my shoulder.

"Shall I make us some food?" He interlaced his fingers with mine tugging me down stairs, happy and content to live in our happy little bubble. I scrambled to get onto the counter as Nox started cooking. I kicked out my feet into the air trying to wiggle on to the counter. "Fuck," Nox whispering, I glanced back at him, he was watching me, well more accurately my ass.

"Here," he commented. He wrapped his hands around my hips lifting me onto the counter, a small growl emanating from his chest. "Beautiful. What would you like to eat?" Nox took a deep breath, rubbing his nose in my hair. "Pancakes, and can I have some potatoes?" I answered smiling.

"Of course," Nox stated as he started to pull out items from the cupboards. I watched as my mate made us food, getting lost admiring his features -the slow way he went about cooking.

Unknown

I watched - concealed in a blanket of shadows, as the guards ran a rogue off the packs land.

Sage

Nox had left for work soon after we finished up breakfast. I found myself back on the couch, staring at the walls. I ran my finger over the dent in the drywall, small cracks radiating out from it, someone had punched the wall at some point.

My attention drifted outside, the birds calling to each other. A small sniffle and whine interrupted the birds. *What was that?*

I ran my hands over the wood of the front door, it was new. Was it safe to go out? It was bright out there. A scent drifted under the door, it was familiar. I had smelt it so many times from those in the other cells. *Fear.* I threw the door open, blinking back the light.

The scent was drifting on the wind from the forest. I ducked my head and barreled into the underbrush. A small child hid behind a large rock. His blonde hair hung obscuring his face. A sniff escaped the small boy. I crouched near him, leaving an opening to his left.

He looked up, his face red, tears streaming down his cheeks. "What are you doing here?" he asked, between tears.

"I came to see if you are okay," I offered.

"I can't find my mom. I'm lost," he sniffed. The child wailed at the top of his small lungs. "I will help you," I offered. I stood up slowly, offering the child my hand. He took it, his hands muddy and sticky. We made our way back to the pack's main town.

Despite all my gusto to help the child, I could not face all the people in the main town square. He didn't find his mother there, so we moved on roaming all throughout the pack looking for her. "Hey! What are you doing with my son!" A young woman was running towards us, before I could pull the boy behind me he ran towards her too. She snarled at me as she tugged him into her arms. She stormed off.

My knees hit the forest floor as she disappeared from view, I tugged myself into the smallest size I could become. I bit my knee lightly. I was only trying to help. *I only wanted to help. I was only trying to help. I only wanted to help. Why? No one wants your useless help.* The crunching of twigs pulled me from my thoughts. I froze waiting -watching- someone was walking by, they passed.

I was only trying to help. I was only trying to help. The hours slipped by unnoticed. The sunset was starting to turn the leaves golden. *Nox.* He would be getting home from work, and I wouldn't be there, he would worry. I don't want to cause him trouble. Tears slipped down my face, he will worry.

I don't want him to worry. I pressed my eyes to my knees,

breathing in deeply, trying to recall Nox's scent from my clothes. There it was. Nox's scent. *Wait.* It was coming from me, he was nearby. My body knocked against something hard. Nox's arms were wrapped around my shaking form. I nuzzled his neck, clinging to his shirt, my knuckles turning white. "I was only trying to help," I wailed.

"It's ok," Nox rubbed my back in slow circles. We walked back in silence, night was falling fast as we reached home. *Home.* I had gone much further than I had expected. It was dark and the stars splattered the sky, shining brightly.

We settled together on the couch, limbs tangled. He peppered my face and neck with gentle kisses, dragging a blanket over the two of us. It felt good to be home, safe in his arms. I looked up at my mate, our noses brushed as I looked over his features. I smiled. "Sage," he breathed, damn near purring my name, sleep loosely gripping his voice. "You are getting so much stronger," he whispered, his voice deep, "so much better with the world." He was quiet for some time as he played with my hair.

I was jolted from my half slumber. Someone was banging on our door. I yanked the blanket over my head, trying to hide from the sound. Chuckling as he went, Nox opened the door. The voice that ranted on as soon as the door opened was the woman who took the boy, presumably his mother.

I tried my best to block out her words. Her tone was harsh and angry. I held the blanket up with my hands, watching as the light from the hall shone through the small holes in the weave of the blanket.

Their voices drifted into the house and to the kitchen. A lot seemed to happen there -so many important conversations. "And now he is missing again!" Her wail echoed around the house. "Tell me what happened from the beginning."

"Well… well.. Maddox ran off," she explained.

"Then..Then.. I found him in the woods, kidnapped by some wolf. She was hiding in the bushes behind him. If I find her, she is getting it! I swear if I see her again!" She slammed against the counter. I stiffened, on high alert.

"And…now he is missing. Again!" the woman shrieked.

"We will find him," Nox soothed.

"I want you to go home and sleep. You need rest. We will find him,"Nox promised.

"I know it's hard," Nox started. The angered wolf huffed but left nonetheless. Nox returned to my side, he didn't try to remove the blanket from my head, instead sliding his hands over my hips pulling me close. "I was only trying to help," I whispered through the blanket.

"What?" He stroked the blanket that was over my head. "He said he was lost. I was only trying to help. We were looking for his mother," I explained. The blanket slid off my face, I did not look at him. "It's ok. You did the right thing," he soothed.

His fingers laced into my hair, pulling me close, he kissed my head. "I want Theo," I hummed.

"I know. We will get him back," he promised.

Sage

I watched as the sun dipped below the trees. The worn wood of the porch scratched against my tights as I shifted. Nox was out with his men looking for the boy. A piece of gravel rolled and bounced off my shoe. I looked up to see the angry mother striding towards me. "I am here to apologize," she stated. I waited looking at her shoes, they were muddy, beat up sneakers. "Alpha Nox, clarified the situation to me. I did not know you could hear me and I did not know you were trying to help. I am sorry." She waited for a response, it never came. She gave up and left after a few minutes.

~

I had not moved from the porch, determined to see him the second he returned home. It was dark, with only the stars to accompany me in his absence. *Is he okay?* He would have come back by now, or sent word that he was going to be late. Maybe someone knew where he was. From my roaming's the other day I had mapped out a lot of the pack's internal territory. I batted at the branches as I made my way to the pack house, *house,* being an inaccurate description. *Hotel? Castle?* Pack house. It was the very heart of the pack, it was the home to many, offices, recreational areas, and a kitchen that never closed and served food to any that wished.

It was a city in itself. The courtyard outside thrummed with people. I slipped between them, jumping out of their way. I went unnoticed as I was batted around like a leaf in the wind as I made my way to the doors.

I stumbled in through the main doors, it was much quieter here. Many people were milling about but I had the space to move freely. I walked around many rooms and halls, looking for Nox or someone I recognized. After I had made my way up nearly ten floors, I found what I have to assume is Nox's office. It smelled like him, and looked office like. *Kind of.* I walked up to the door.

"You can't go in there without permission," someone mentioned to me as they passed by me in the hall. Nox would be okay with it right? He shared his bed with me. I could visit his office, couldn't I? *Nox .* I pulled on the door, no one else stopped me.

I stepped into the room, there were several people in here. None were Nox. *Where was he?* Every single eye jumped to me, staring. I backed up, my back hit the door, it snapped shut. *Stop looking at me. Who were they?* I slide down the door, hugging my knees. Nox. I wanted Nox. *Nox. NOX!* One of the men crouched down in front of me, his face blurry.

"You okay?" His voice was distorted. The other men came closer and stood behind him. I rocked back and forth. "What's wrong? Is she ok?" he asked.

"I don't know. Fuck. If only Nox was here," the other cursed. Nox's name snapped me back to the room. "Nox?" I looked up at them. Where was he? "Oh shit," one of them hissed.

"She doesn't know…" someone whispered.

"She is his mate and she doesn't know what happened," they talked as if I wasn't here.

"Do we tell her?" one asked.

"She is fragile. No," the other answered.

"She is going to keep looking for him, and asking questions. What do we tell her?" they argued.

"She will figure it out eventually," one offered.

"She is his mate. Our future Luna. We have to tell her," the other said decisively.

"Hey," one of them said softly, now talking to me and not between themselves. "Nox is missing." *Missing? How? Where?* Tears raced down my cheeks dripping onto my legs. I battled my lungs to draw breath. One of them tried to rub my shoulders similarly to how Nox would have,I pulled away -the touch was anything but soothing.

As my breathing made way to gasping then whimpering, then howling, they just stood there watching me, shocked. "What do we do?" one asked, watching me.

"Without Nox? Nothing," the other said. *Nox.* I bolted, bashing through the door, and down the hall. Away from everything. I just wanted Nox. I slammed out the main door and into the wide world, barreling into the trees. I gasped leaning against a small tree, panting, the world spinning. *What happened to Nox?*

He was not dead, or gravely injured, I would have been able to feel it through the wisp of a bond we have. Even though the mating bond is not sealed it is still there. I needed to be in his arms.

I don't know how long it took me to right the world again. Once I could see clearly and move without losing which direction the sky was, I made my way back to Nox's office. As I re-entered the city around the pack house, weaving my way back to the courtyard. There were more and more people around than before.

Someone walked into me, knocking me to the floor. I stood up brushing the dirt off my clothes and tugging them back into place. I fight my way around people avoiding getting knocked to the floor again. I wait outside the office door. I step inside once again. The same group of men stood in it.

"How? Where?" I gasped gripping the door knob, fighting to stay upright. The room started to swirl, into a mess of colours.

"He was out with the guard, there were reports of rogues. They have trapped him." The glare he got for the answer he gave, made my shudder. "Why did you tell her?" the other snapped.

"Would you want this information withheld about your mate?" the other countered.

"How.. Do we get him back?" I fought my stutter to get my words out.

"Come have a look at this." He pointed to Nox's desk. A patchwork of maps littered the top. "They are in this area, stuck between this pack, which we can not enter, and their camp here." His fingers pointed out each area marked with a pin as he talked.

"We are sending a group of guards, who will flank the rogues from the other side, and that should be enough support to get them home," he explained.

"I am going with them," I announce.

"We can't let you," they responded at the same time. *No!*

"I am going," I repeated.

"If you stay out of the fighting and with a guard, you could come to the border," one offered.

"Okay," I agreed.

"We will come to keep you safe," one stated.

"Fine," I narrowed my eyes at him. "Look. It's the best we can do," he said, raising his hands.

"We can't take our Luna into a dangerous situation, especially to rescue our Alpha. Let alone what Nox would do if you were hurt," he explained.

"We will get you as close as we can," he offered. As a unit we moved out -one of them in front of me, one behind. We joined up with the guard unit, they were preparing to head out.

Nox

Sage was eating better and better. I shifted around the maps on my desk. I had considered getting a home office to be closer to her, but people would come by to talk to me all the time. I liked having my own space away from the pack, and I liked that it was now our space.

I need to work though. As much as I wanted to stay home and spend it with her I was the Alpha of this pack. I wanted to stay in our house, in our bedroom, in our bed, *in her.* I couldn't. *"James. Jake. My office."* I linked. The rogues were a danger to my pack and my mate, we were dealing with them today. "Nox!" Jake shouted as he and James sauntered in. "The threat these rogues are causing ends today," I announced.

"So we are in a fuck around mood today," Jake smirked.

"They took a pup… and my mate's pet," I stated.

"Shit," Jake hissed.

"From all the reports, their camp is in this area. We will take them from here," I stated as I pointed to the map.

"That's very close to Garrot's pack," James noted

"We will have to be careful to avoid his land," Jake added.

"Ok, so we take some guards out and smoke-em." Jake may act like a child ninety percent of the time, but he was my third for a reason, at this moment I just needed to remember why. "I will go," I announced.

"Alpha…" James never thought it was a good idea for me to leave the pack.

"You two will stay here to keep everyone safe. Including my mate. Especially my mate," I ordered.

"I will get them ready." Jake left, he understood why I must go. I spent much of my days useless to Sage, at least now I could protect her pack and her. As a group we moved out, shifting to our wolves.

Running as a unit through the woods, as we left our packs borders a couple wolves peeled off running parallel to the main group. Every wolf had their eyes, ears and nose on high alert.

Nothing, mile after mile, still nothing. With each passing mile I grow more and more nervous. Something wasn't right. We were approaching Garrot's border, I pulled the unit along the border running down along the neutral passage.

I halted, everyone in the unit stopping behind me. A black

rabbit sat in the middle of the clearing. It looked like Theo, but it was a black rabbit. They all look very similar. It smelled like Theo, but Theo smelled like all rabbits. I snapped my fingers at it taking a couple steps forward. It was enough to scare off any rabbit, but it looked right at me, even taking a small step forward, then hopping forward. It was Theo -I am sure of it.

I darted forward, and scooped up the small animal in my mouth. I paused, a twig snapped, the wind stirred. I swirled around. Beneath the shadows of the bushes -something glowed. A set of eyes. A small unit of scraggly thin wolves appeared from the leaves. *"More behind us,"* one of my wolves linked me.

My chest rumbled, the leaves themselves curling back from my growl. I locked eyes with their leader, holding his gaze. Every muscle in my body is a live wire, ringing with energy. Hunter and hunted. It was just a matter of who was which. This is not good. I watched, not moving. I gently placed the rabbit back down. The leader took a step forward, the unmistakable snapping of his shift broke the silence.

"Shift," he snapped. I shifted back, to my human form -naked. I glared at the leader, the fact that we were both naked bothered no one.

~

It was dark now, and our silent stalemate continued. The pack would be worried by now that we had not returned. We needed to end this, but we were outnumbered. Fighting out was not an option, it risked too many lives -I would return to her.

A guttural gasp broke the tense silence, I swirled around as a rogue crashed to the forest floor. Another unit of our guard stood behind him. A wicked smile graced my face -an even playing field.

I turned to the leader, pulling back my fist. I connected with his jaw -the crunch echoed. The fight was quick and brutal -we lost no one. Most of them retreated before we could take them with us. We got a couple though.

We made our way back to our borders, as one group. James and Jake stood just after the boundary line, beside each other, arms crossed. *Whatever they are doing here?* I know things did not go as planned but they would not have left the pack. *Would they?* I shifted back to my human form, barely. "Why did you leave the pack?" I asked.

"We haven't." Jake pointed to the border, which technically they were still on our land. "Even so," I snapped.

"Orders," Jake answered, smiling.

"From who?!" I demanded.

"Our Luna," Jake answer. Sage ducked out from behind them. *Sage . Mate.* She was safe. I took a step towards her, I stopped at the flush that rose in her cheeks. Right. Naked. "Like the view?" I smiled at her. James snorted at me, turning away.

"What? Don't like the view?" I laughed at him. "Nothing I haven't seen before, but I am sure your mate wants some privacy while she enjoys the view." He had a point. Sage's flush was evident enough of how she felt about this. Embarrassed and uncomfortable.

"Let's go home." I wrapped my arms around her, bringing her close. Her scent. *Oh. Goddess help me.* Not everyone didn't already know she was my mate at this point; it would have been obvious in my own body's reaction. My cock hard, pressed against her side.

Her flush deepened, her heart racing. *Oh how delightful.* Her reaction for me was ego boosting. I kissed her forehead, resting my forehead to hers. "Later. I promise." It was a mere whisper for her ears only. She licked her lips, and smiled at me. *Fuck.* "I missed you," she whispered.

"I missed you too," I reciprocated.

"Let's get back. So you two can get a room," James smirked at me. *"Getting lucky!"* Jake sang down the link. I growled at him down the link. Sage tugged at me, wanting to get home.

"Wait." I smiled at her eagerness to get me home. *Oh I hope she tugs me all the way home to our bedroom.* "I think he missed you." I grabbed Theo from the hands of my men. He was naked too, I tried not to let that bother me, she wasn't looking at him at all. She was looking at me. *Me. Her mate.* I gently placed Theo in her hands.

She looked up at me with tears in her eyes. My mate, my small traumatized mate stood on her toes, to press her lips to mine. She kissed me, in front of my people. Our people. *Fuck.* She would not be able to keep up with us, and she could not shift. I leaned over to whisper in her ear.

"You are going to ride home on my back," I informed. She nodded, tucking Theo in her shirt. *Lucky rabbit. Oh what I would give to be in her shirt.* I shifted to my wolf, skipping around to let her get on my back. She looked at me wide eyed. It was bad decorum to ride on another wolf. "Nox?" I licked at her ankles. She huffed at me, and swung her leg over my back. *Okay maybe bad decorum, but the weight of her was delightful.*

I dropped Sage off at home, promising to be back. *Fuck.* I ached to be near her, but the pack cells waited for me. I walked to the pack's cells. My people were tossing our guests into their rooms. "Alpha," they greeted.

"Will you be questioning them now?" I looked down at them, my body twitching, the rage bubbling up my spine. "If I question them now I will probably kill them and get nothing. I need to be with my mate right now." They nodded and I left. Sage was upstairs playing with Theo on our bedroom floor. "Beautiful," I whispered into her hair.

"You should get some sleep," I said.

"With you," she added. *Fuck.*

"You know that it has two meanings, don't you?" I asked.

"What is the other one?" she questioned.

"Never mind." We curled up in bed together, holding her close as she slowly drifted to sleep. I could never tire of this. Soon I joined her, dreaming of the other meaning to her words. *Sleep with me.*

~

I had some beef with my boys. Letting her come with them? *Really?* Once their asses had been handed to them, it was back to my mate. I was not leaving her side for a week. They were both seated at my desk as I got there. Joking and laughing. *Idiots.* "What's up?" Jake said, spinning in my chair. "Out!" I pointed at my chair with my finger, and flicked it through the air. He jumped from the chair going quiet. "Why was Sage there?" I growled.

"Look, we are sorry." Jake raised his hands in the air shrugging. *Come on dude do better.* "She is our Luna. She made her wishes clear. Were we to disobey her?" James pointed out.

"If you ever pull a stunt like that again; I will rip off your balls and nail them to your door," I snarled at them. Jake went white at the threat and lowered his gaze. James held my eye contact before slowly lowering his too. There was an awkward silence that went on far too long. "She's getting better with the whole talking and people thing," Jake offered up. "If you need me. Don't bother, I will be with Sage." I smiled at them before leaving my office.

Sage was awake and sitting up in bed. She had rearranged all the blankets into a little nest around her. "Good morning." I pulled at one of the blankets to get into bed with her, she gave me a look of pure annoyance.

"Sorry. Permission to come aboard?" I asked, smiling. She gave me a look of confusion.

"May I join you?" She stuck her tongue out at me, I gave her the smile of a devil. She flushed at me -*fuck*-I climbed over the bed wrapping her in my arms. "You are tempting me," I practically purred into her hair. "Nox." I kissed her temple. I could feel her heartbeat on my skin. *She was so beautiful.* She nuzzled into me, her ass rubbing up my thigh. *Fuck.*

"Sage," I growled, nipping at the back of her neck. My hands drifted to her hips, gripping them lightly. I pulled her hips to mine. Rubbing up against her. Her breathing hitched. *Delicious.*

Sage

"Hungry?" I was getting my appetite back, which Nox seemed to be happy with, but the guilt of eating still sat heavy with me. "Can we have something with cheese?" I watched Nox as he went about making us food. I watched the way his muscles flexed under his shirt. *If only he wasn't wearing one.* The smooth, assured way, he moved about the room. While he was waiting for our food to finish cooking he made up a plate of greens to give to Theo. Nox didn't really like Theo that much, but the care he took of him for me was outstanding.

Nox looked up at me, his smile was dazzling, all the seriousness of his title gone. He was a young male making food for his mate, nothing more nothing less. I wish I could take some of the weight off his shoulders. Why can't I? *Because you are broken and useless, you would make things worse.* "Nox?" He stopped and turned to me, wiping his hands clean on a towel. "Yes," he hummed.

"I…. never mind," I started.

"It's ok, you don't have to tell me. You can if you want to, but you don't have to," he soothed. *I want to help. You… And the pack.* "Later?" I asked.

"Okay," he hummed. I waited, but Nox just kept making food. "Grilled cheese," he said as he placed a plate in front of me. I wrinkled my nose at it. I picked up the warm bread, cheese dripping out from between it. "Eat up. I have to go to work soon," Nox added before he kissed my forehead, a matching sandwich. I wrinkled my nose at Nox. *Why did he have to go? I* had no plans for the day, the hours would stretch into days. *Alone.* "I don't want to be alone," I whispered.

"You don't have to be. I can ask Fin to come by," he offered. *Fin? Who?* "I don't want a stranger," I complain.

"He's not a stranger. He took care of you while I was gone."

"Which time?" *Why was I angry? He* was trying to help, it wasn't his fault he had responsibilities. "Sage. I'm sorry," Nox whispered. Nox wrapped my shaking body in his arms. "Mate," he hummed. It was only a whisper, but it quieted the growl that was building in my ribs. "I promise I will return to you," he vowed.

"I am yours," he promised. My heart pounded, no possessive Alpha growling, no 'do as I say'. No orders. He was nothing like the Alpha's I met before. He does not delight in pain, or his people submitting to him.

"Ours," Nox leaned down and kissed me, soft gentle brushes of his lips, back and forth across my lips, then down my jaw. "Ours," he whispered into my hair. His fingers combed through my hair slowly. "I want to help," I admit.

"With what?" he asked.

"The weight on your shoulders," I answered. Nox nuzzled the side of my face, drawing in a breath through his nose. "You know some of the pack already call you Luna," he revealed.

"I am your mate…. That is what a Luna is…" I trailed off.

"No. Luna is so much more." *What?* She was just the mate to the Alpha, there to make an heir. "She leads with the Alpha, as a pair," Nox added. *Leads?* "You don't have to. You can just be my mate," Nox soothed.

"I want to," I pressed on. Did I want this? *Yes. With him.* "What do I have to do?" I asked.

"The pack has to officially accept you as Luna, and there is some ceremonial bullshit. But other than that we can figure it out together," Nox whispered. I nodded against his hand, as it rested on my cheek. A knock ended our conversion. It was Fin, he was here. "Alpha. Luna." He shifted around nervously. "I …. I have to take care of my sister today. I hope that it is ok that I brought her with me," Fin explained. *No. No more people. Not very Luna of you.* Nox looked down at me, waiting. I nodded looking at his feet.

"Thank you Luna," Fin sighed. I walked back inside the house, sinking onto the couch. Nox came in after me, and tucked a blanket around me. "You could have said no," he breathed into my hair, kissing my head. "I know."

"Hello." A high cheery voice squealed. *No. NO. Make it stop.* "Nice kitchen!" The voice twittered on for a while. Didn't even greet her Alpha. Or say goodbye when he leaves with a promise to return soon. "Can we bake something?" *If you could cook he wouldn't have to do all the work.* "Yes," I answered. I pulled myself from the cocoon of warmth Nox had made for me. She squealed and clapped her hands jumping about.

"Please calm down," Fin said from the door, always the guard. "What shall we make?" she asked.

"Cake," I exclaimed. I was craving something sweet. She squealed even louder, my hands clapping over my ears. "Jezra!" Fin snapped at her. I looked at her face, taking in every detail. *Jezra.* I turned to Fin, taking in him as well. *Fin.* I will learn who everyone is. *My pack.*

Jezra started to pull ingredients out of the cupboards talking through each one. Step by step she walked me through the process. Starting with mixing the flour, salt, baking powder, and cacao in one bowl, then moving to the next. In went eggs, milk, and two different sugars.

The hours slipped by as we worked through all the steps of making a cake. As we watched the cake bake, I repeated them over and over in my head. I will make Nox a cake all by myself.

Nox

My brain was fogged up after hours of paperwork. I needed to clear my head. I knew one sure fire way to do that. *Her.* "I'm going home." I gripped James and Jake's shoulders as a goodbye. "Me too." James dropped the paperwork he was doing and stood to follow me. "I'm gonna stay a little longer." Jake was still pouring over his stake of papers. His was still double what ours were, and he had significantly less to do, but he was not great at paperwork. Though he tried, probably harder than either of us did, he still got all of his done, *somehow.*

James and I walked out of the office, nodding and greeting each wolf we walked by, occasionally stopping to chat. A quick *'how are you'* or *'how are the pups'* or some other nicety. The ties my pack had ran back generations and would run for generations to come.

James peeled off towards his home, leaving me to walk in peace the half of the way to my home. My mate -I gave the door a light knock before walking in. Sage was standing in the middle of the hallway, she stared at me wide eyed. She had not expected to be caught in the hall.

She was covered in flour, from head to toe. She let out a small squeak before running to me, throwing her arms around me. "Stay," she commanded and then disappeared into the kitchen. A hushed conversation rattled between her and the other people in the kitchen.

"Alpha," Jezra greeted me, she had not earlier and had most likely earned a scolding from Fin. Fin was all but pushing her from the house. "Alpha. She says you can go in." He tilted his to the kitchen. I nodded at him, before walking to my waiting mate. *Sage.*

I found her sitting on the counter, her hands behind her back. The room around her was equally covered in flour, and some other baking ingredients, at least two eggs were smashed on the floor. The smile that beamed from her could have lit up the world had it known to watch her. The fact that she could smile. To see her feeling happy with every inch of her being. It lit something deep in me. *Home. Safe.* I slowly walked up to her savoring this moment, committing it to memory. I placed my hands either side of her, getting lost in her eyes. *Mine.*

"I made it for you," she explained. She pulled a large, lumpy chocolate cake from behind her back. I ran a finger through the thick frosting. I reached out and rubbed the tip of my frosting covered finger over her nose. She wrinkled her nose at the frosting on it. I smiled at her, and she smiled back at me. Every smile is a gift, handcrafted just for me. I leaned down and licked the frosting off her nose. "Nox!" she squealed.

"Sage," I replied.

"You are my home. My other half," I breathed in her scent. She was like taking the first breath of air. I had not known I was drowning without her. It was like I had been looking at the night sky my whole life, not a single star to be found, then she opened my eyes, and there were constellations everywhere.

Sage

Nox had settled us in front of the TV, I sat on his lap. I fiddled with the edge of the blanket. Pulling at the loose thread. "You are stressed." Nox fingers stilled in my hair.

"Don't worry about it," he mused.

"I will," I pointed out.

"Sage. It's my burden," he reassured.

"You are my mate," I pointed out. His fingers resumed their gentle stroking of my hair. This would be a fight for another day. "I want more cake," I stated.

"You should eat something with nutrition in it," Nox reminded me.

"Please," I begged.

"Please don't pout," Nox groaned.

"Cake," I begged, I made sure to deepen my pout. "A small one," he conceded.

"Thank you," I replied as he handed me a plate with a small slice on it. I picked up the fork, scoping some of the cake up. "Open," I instructed. Nox took the bite I was offering him. I licked my plate clean before setting it on the table. I leaned towards him, kissing him gently on the lips. He tasted like chocolate cake. I licked his lips, smiling at him.

"Do I taste good?" He smiled at me, lust burning in his eyes. Curling my fingers into his shirt as his hands gripped my hips. "Mine," he growled nipping at my shoulder. Our little bubble was shattered by a knock. I jumped back from Nox darting behind the couch. Nox wrapped a blanket around my shoulders, before walking to the door.

The door opened, whoever was at the door was not invited in. They were talking, their voices were hushed, and pained. *What was going on?* The door finally closed and two sets of feet came down the hall. I wiggled my toes under the couch. "Is your mate here?" The disgust dripping from her voice was plain as day. "Yes. Mother." Nox was not having it. *His mother.* His mother snorted, shifting around the room.

"Why do you hate her?" I asked.

"She is weak," she responded.

"What does it matter? She is stronger than you give her credit!" Nox's temper was rising. "She is going to weaken this pack. My pack," she snarled at him. *Watch your tone with my mate!*

"This is my pack now. I am Alpha. She is my mate. It's not about her strength, but our strength together. As a team!" Nox snarled. The crunching of something breaking shot through my memory.

I tilted my head back, retreating into my mind. *I am not here.I am not here. I am not here. Chains dragging on the floor, footsteps following it. A snarl echoing off the walls. The chain was lifted off the floor. Everything went white as the chain slammed down next to my head.*

~

Fingers drifted softly over my hair. I opened my eyes slowly. It was bright. *It's not the cell.* Nox wrapped his arms around me, whispering in my ear. *How long has it been?* I took a deep breath, looking at him. I moved slowly pulling myself from his arms.

"Sage," Nox's voice cracked, he sounded broken, sad but hopeful. He pulled me back into his lap, crushing my ribs as he held me. I wrapped my arms around his neck, nuzzling him, breathing in his scent. "I love you," I whispered.

"I love you too Sage," he repeated.

"Weak," snarled his mother. *She was still here.* "Leave her alone," Nox may not have snarled or yelled, but the authority he spoke with left no room for questions. My muscles twitched. *Run. Get away.* I stayed where I was, gripping his shirt. Nox's mother left. "I'm sorry," Nox apologized.

"I don't want to be seen as weak," I admitted.

"You are not," he reassured me.

"That's all other people see," my voice trembles.

"It's not important," Nox soothed.

"It is to me," I whined.

"Ok," Nox sighed.

"Now," I stated.

"Now what?" he asked.

"Start," I responded.

"You want to start now? How do you want to start?" Nox asked.

"I don't know," I mumbled. *I'm not sure..*

"How about we go for a walk around the pack town," Nox suggested.

"Okay." I stood up and walked to the front door. "You need shoes," he commented. Nox darted upstairs to grab shoes. I looked down and wiggled my toes. I fluffed and tugged at my hair, trying to undo the tangles Nox had made in it. I looked in the mirror. *I looked like a drowned rat*. I tugged a little harder at the tangles. "You look good," Nox commented as he reappeared behind me, shoes swinging in his hands. "It's tangled," I whined. Nox started to pull at my hair, it took him less then a minute to get my hair to lay flat. He placed a kiss on my head, looking at me in the mirror. "We don't have to do this now," he reminded me.

"I want to," I say more to myself.

"You are so brave," Nox cooed.

"I'm terrified," I admit.

"That's what makes you so brave," he commented. I slipped my hand in his, as he guided me out the house. I looked up from the ground, the sun glaring at me. I blinked back the sting -I tried to bat the light away from my face.

Nox

She made it two feet from the house before she was curled up in a ball. "What's wrong?" I ran my hands over her back. "It's so bright," she babbled. She waved her hand in front of her face fighting something she couldn't touch.

"I will be right back." I returned with sunglasses. I gently slid them over her eyes. It took her a moment but she slowly uncurled. I kissed the top of her head. I offered her my hand to help her stand up. She smiled at me, as she refused my hand and stood up on her own. She looked up at me waiting.

"This way," I guided. I offered her my hand again, this time she took it. Every couple of steps she added a little hop to her step. *Cute.* She let go of my hand and twirled around on her toes, then she leaned back and fell into my arms.

I picked her up and swung her around in two circles before setting her feet. *Holy shit. Her laugh.* I gaped at her, the music that was her laugh, a song from her hitting all the notes of my soul. I pulled her to me, feeling her body vibrate against me, the feeling of touching a speaker, not just hearing the song, but feeling it in my bones. She was laughing so hard she sank to the ground. Her laugh was a drug and I was an addict.

Her laugh lit me up, every nerve in my body, glowing with her soul. The fact that she could laugh after everything. *Fuck.* I flopped down on the ground next to her as her laugh faded from sound, but into a glow in her eyes. I pulled her close, nuzzling up to her.

"Where do you want to go? Pack house or the greens?" I asked. The light in her eyes from her laugh lingered as a ghostly sparkle. *Beautiful.* "House," she answered.

"Okay."

"I love you," I whispered.

"I love you too," she replied. We made our way slowly to the pack house, slowly she lost the light in her eyes, as we got closer her anxiety got higher and higher. She shut down more and more. By the time we got to the pack house steps she was nearly curled in a ball. "What now?" She mumbled.

"It's up to you. We can go home or we can go inside," I offered. I focused solely on her. Several people tried to get my attention, but I blocked them out. "Alpha?"

"Sorry I'm busy, if you need something ask James," I repeated , not looking up.

"I will come back another time," they replied, I glanced up.

"Sorry. I'm just with my mate right now," I mention. I looked back at Sage. He nodded at me, smiling at my mate, before leaving. Sage was muttering to herself. *Was this too much too soon?*

Sage

Why did I agree to this? "Sage?" Nox questioned.

"I'm good," I responded.

"You sure?" he questioned.

"Yes," I rocked back and forth. People were coming to talk to Nox and he was turning them away. *Why?* "Don't turn them away," I begged.

"I'm here for you right now and only you," he reassured.

"They need their Alpha," I pushed.

"My mate needs me right now," he pressed. *But did I need him more than they did right now?* I stood up, my knees shaking, I offered Nox my hand. He smiled at me, and took my hand. He slowly guided me through the doors into the main hall. *I could do this. Right? With him. Yes.*

I walked slowly down the hall, placing one foot gently in front of the other. My heel brushed my toes on the other foot, inching down the hall. Finally I made it to the first doorway. I peeked my head around the door frame, it was a living room. There were a bunch of people lounging around the room, and as my head came into view they all looked up at me. I pulled back, heart hammering. Nope this was too much. *I'm done.* "Can we go home?" I pleaded.

"Yes." Nox ran his hand down my back. "Alpha?" someone asked him.

"Yes?" he hummed.

"Is this your mate? Sorry. I heard a rumour," The man that stood before us, was tall and muscled, I fought the urge to step back from him. Nox was with me. *I would be ok.* This is my pack too now. They were like them. They are not them. *I am safe.* "Yes," Nox replied. Nox pulled me against him. My back flush with his chest, his warmth seeping into my skin -ground me.

"Sage. This is Seth -he is Jake's mate," he explained. Jake...*Nox's third... I've met him.* Seth, I took a moment to take him in. "Luna. Nox. Seth," Jake greeted coming up behind Seth, his hand resting on his shoulder.

"Jake," Seth tutted and kissed his cheek. *Cute.* "When is your Luna Ceremony gonna be?" *My what?* I looked at Seth, Jake and lastly at Nox. "Still planning it," Nox replied, not missing a beat -I frowned at Nox. "Good to see you Seth, I will see you at tomorrow meeting?" Nox ushered me out the door. I waited till we were almost home before opening my mouth.

"What's a Luna Ceremony?" I asked.

"It is… a ceremony where the Alpha's mate is.. presented to the pack and .. the pack decides if they accept her as Luna. As the female half to the pack leadership…" He seemed to pick his words carefully.

II

Spirit

Sage

Nox was working non-stop to find Maddox, *Dox*. Having one of the pack's pups missing was up-ending the pack. Everyone was stressed -the future of the pack was endangered. Nox worked round the clock following up leads, hunting down information, and executing search parties. With each day that Dox was missing the stress built and it was getting to the pack, people were starting to question Nox's leadership.

It was hard to watch him fight this one on his own. A piece of him was breaking as he failed to protect his pack. He would not let me help. *Not that I could.* He spent all day at his pack office, then when he got home, he would spend another couple hours in his home office.

I ran my fingers down the wall, walking towards his home office. I don't think he will be mad if I go into his office to help, right? When has he ever been mad at me? *They always get mad at you.* I gently pressed my fingers to the door, it swung out from under my hand. The lights were off, but the large window lit the door. His desk was covered in papers.

I scanned the desk for somewhere to start. It was nonsense,

reports, and maps intermingled with pages of notes. I smiled at his loopy scrawling print, it was the visual representation of his voice. One particular note caught my eye. It was made with three different colours of green, unlike the plain black of the rest.

It was my name. *Sage.* Over and over my name was written all over the page, in a chaotic jumble, not following the lines on the page, some big, some small, different styles, some had sharp lines, some little curls. In between each one had little hearts. *What does this have to do with Dox?* I quickly folded the piece of paper up and tucked it in my waistband. *Would he notice?*

The gentle clink of the front door unlocking reached my ears. I bolted from his office letting the door gently swing close, but not latch. I darted to the kitchen, the paper in my waistband itching at my skin.

He was going to be so mad that I was in his office. *And took something.* He would know the second I moved, he would hear the rustle of the paper. *Hide.* The door opened, and closed. Was it Nox at the door? He normally greeted me, but it was silent. *Hide.* I ran over to the island in the middle of the kitchen. The large cupboards on the island were empty. I slipped inside, closing it behind me, using my hand to hold the door so it would not make a sound. I held my breath, and listened to the footsteps getting closer. "Sage?" Nox called.

"Sage?!" Nox was getting panicked, his footsteps getting fast, looping the room, then leaving. It was Nox. He was here. *Safe.*

I pushed on the cupboard door, cracking it open, letting light into the cupboard. "Sage," Nox called. The lights flicked off as Nox knelt before the door. I wrapped my fingers around the edge of the door, Nox's fingers brushed against them, wrapping them around mine.

"What happened?" He choked out the words around his extended canines -quietly. He was scared. I looked up and one of his eyes was visible in the crack. His eyes were slowly turning from yellow to his usual blue. The deep unending blue *-of Nox*, of my mate. Not the yellow of a panicked possessive Alpha. "Nox," I breathed.

"What happened? I couldn't find you," he panted.

"I was in your office. I'm sorry," I grovel.

"Ok. What happened?" Nox pulled my fingers off the door, holding them gently. "Are you mad?" I whispered. Nox yanked the door wide open. "Why would I be?" he asked.

"It's your space. It's your office," I explained.

"You can go anywhere in our house." *Our house.* "Come here beautiful." Nox gently tugged on my wrist. I climbed out of my little hole and into his waiting arms. The paper in my waistband crinkled as his hand ran over it. Now he will be mad. "And I took this," I admitted. I pulled the paper out and handed it to him. "Oh. This. I can explain…" He nervously rubbed his neck. "I was…thinking…" he rubbed his neck shifting around. He was embarrassed about it. "About you." He smiled at me sheepishly. I pulled the paper from his hand, bringing it to my heart smiling at him. "That's cute," I whispered.

"I'm glad you find it amusing," he laughed, throwing his head back letting the sound fill the room. He quieted as he looked at me for a long time. "I want to be clear -you are my mate, there is very little you can do that I won't love. You can go anywhere, do anything, and as long as I know you are safe. I am happy. I do not own you. You can choose anything, and I choose you. There are no lines I will not cross with you. And if you do make me mad, I will talk to you. You. Are. My. Mate. My other half," Nox proclaimed.

Nox

I had not slept much through the night, Sage was having nightmares, and would wake every half an hour not knowing where she was. It wasn't until the sun started to rise that she got any sleep. I brushed the hair from her face, the circles under her eyes a deep purple.

I pulled her close to my body, the weight of her grounding me. Her sweaty limbs were flung over mine, her skin warm. I was concerned about her, she was back peddling, or maybe she was healing. Maybe this is what healing looks like, maybe she was accepting her broken part back into herself, or maybe she is getting re-traumatized.

I need advice.

~

I rocked on my feet, debating if I wanted to hear the answer to my questions. *Fuck it.* "Come in my son," my mother called, she stood in the door frame smiling. "I love you mother," I said as I hugged her tight, her sweater warm, smelling of childhood. "I love you too," she cooed.

"I need advice," I stated.

"Come in," she offered.

"What is it Nox?" We sat in her private living room, on the second level, it was full of many clashing floral prints. "Why do you hate Sage?" *Did she see something I did not?* "I don't hate Sage." *Bullshit.* "I know what it takes to be Luna. It will break her." *What?*

It will break her. Slowly my soul shattered. I had not thought of what it would do to her." She is stronger than you think," I begged.

"It's not about strength. She can't just fight through this. She is not a Luna, it is not something you become or learn, it is something you are," my mother stated, coldly.

"Mother," I growled.

"It's the truth. I should know. This is my pack too. I was Luna for over 30 years," she chided.

"I think she is exactly what this pack needs, what I need as a leader," I argued.

"She will not be a good Luna," she repeated.

"She is my mate, she will be the Luna of my pack. I am not taking another as Luna," I snarled.

"Nox," my mother hissed.

"Just give her a chance," I begged.

"Fine. Is she busy right now?" she asked.

"Yes. You should come by next week though," I offered.

"I will see you both next week then. I love you Nox," she sighed.

"I love you too Mother." I fiddled with the poppy print blanket, as we sat in a somewhat awkward silence.

"Are you taking her to the dance?" *Dance?* I completely forgot about that.

"Yes," I answered.

Sage

It was cold, despite the wild fire that Nox was. The night was a dark blanket gently weighing down on me, weighted with memories, it was equally comforting and suffocating. I was at home, but it still rubbed my soul the wrong way sending anxious shivers up my spine. The night was my home, the darkness was my enemy.

I looked out the window to the star spattered sky. The stars glittered and winked at me, the night around them turning to smoke, drifting over the stars. It twisted through the window, swirling around my outstretched hand, wrapping around my wrist. It whispered to me. *Just let go. I'm here. Child.*

I glanced around as the smoke pooled on the floor and sprouted trees around me -ghost trees. I slid out of bed, my toes sliding across the floor, but instead of the wooden floor of our bedroom, the soft texture of grass met my touch. I looked back at our bed, it was gone. Nox was gone, I was in a dark ghostly world, alone. Not an ounce of colour marred the trees or ground.

"Child," The voice was soft, coming from the world around me.

It was ethereal, soft and light. *Was it really even there?* "Child," the voice repeated from behind me. A ghost stood before me. A woman, all white except for her hair, which was pale blue. Her eyes had no iris, no pulp, just white. Her clothes were just fabric that seemed to float around her body, drifting in the same invisible breeze that drifted through her hair. The little wisps of night intermingle with her bone white locks. The breeze danced around the two of us. She smelt like dreams and starlight.

She lifted one slender hand up towards me pointing at me with her finger. The long white nail filed to a point, her elbow bent, then dropping back to her side. "I'm sorry," she whispered.

Tears were rolling down her face, dropping to the ground where they exploded into little pin pricks of starlight. Her translucent milky white tears kept falling as she spoke. "I hope you heal each other my child." I blinked and the stars outside the window twinkled back at me. *What was that? Who was she?*

I rolled over and nuzzled my nose into Nox's back, my face was damp. I swiped the tears off of my cheeks, they glowed faintly of moon light. Sleep gently caressing my brain with supple fingers before I slipped back to sleep. My dreams are haunted by a ghostly moon hidden by a blanket of black clouds.

Sage

Nox burst through the front door with a whirlwind of emotion, he had a wild look in his eye. *What's wrong?* I sat up at the sound of Nox thundering up the stairs. I pulled the blanket off of my legs as he blundered into our room. "Hello, little one." He flopped on the bed next to me forcing an air of casual calm he was not feeling. I shifted Theo out of the way. Despite his chaotic energy I smiled at my mate. "How is Theo?" he asked.

"Good," I answered.

"We are going shopping," he announced. He stood up smiling at me, offering me his hand to help me up. "What for?" I took his hand, he pulled me to my feet before bringing me to his arms. "A dress," he stated. *A dress?*

"For you." *For me?* No, I did not need a new dress. "I don't…." I started pulling out of his arms to look him in the eye. "You do. We are. It will be fun," He left no room for argument, but he had a pleading look in his eye. This clearly meant something to him. What I did not know. "Nothing crazy," I said pointedly.

"Let's go!" He pulled me back into his arms, lifting me slightly as he twirled me around. There was nothing like the trust it took to give over to the disorientation of flying through the air, but he had it. "I need to change." I skipped over to our shared closet. I skipped down the stairs -two at a time. Nox was waiting by the door -on his phone, working. He's always working. I pulled on my shoes, ignoring the burst of pain as I tugged too violently. Jumping to my feet to force the heels all the way on.

"Ready to go?" He asked not looking up from his phone. "Yes!" He looked up at me -taking in my clothes. He blinked slowly, the fire in his eyes burning my skin. "Trying to tempt me?" I blushed under his gaze. *Yes.* I swung my hips side to side making my skirt float around my hips. "Later. I will show you how good it looks on the floor," He whispered in my ear his voice near a growl. "But now...we will find you a dress fit for the queen you are," he whispered. I am no queen. *But maybe I was his.*

Though the car was cool with the windows down, it was nothing but steamy. Between the way Nox was looking at me and the slow circles his thumb was making on my thigh it was a miracle we made it to the small shop.

Nox took a moment to temper the fire in his eyes once we were in the parking lot.

"My mother wants to spend some time with you." *What?* The fire and steam gone in an instant. "I pushed it back to next week," he noted.

"I had a weird dream," I confessed. I felt the need to share something as well.

"What about?" He looked over at me and smiled, the small ticking sounds of the car cooling down. I shook my head, looking at the floor of the car.

"Shall we?" He angled his head towards the small store we were parked in front of. It was a two story building. The balcony above had a small jungle of plants hanging off of it. Nox jogged round to my side before I could open the door myself, opening it for me. A gentle kiss to my cheek before he slipped his hand in mine as we entered the store.

"Hello," an older lady greeted us, she was smiling, her curly hair bouncing as she glided towards us. She wore a long skirt, and a long sleeve blouse, both looked unfathomable soft looking. The store was a jumble of colours, dress after dress hung on rows and rows of racks. "Dear, what can I help you with?" She had moved from the back of the store and appeared next to Nox, talking to him. I jumped, scuttling behind a dress rack. *Stupid. Stupid. How did she get there?*

"I'm so sorry," I mumbled. I yanked the skirt of the closest dress over my head, sinking to the floor. *I thought we were past this?* Past everything sending me back here. But no, I was back in that cell, waiting for the first blow. The skirt was lifted from my head. Nox smiled at me offering his hand, the lady hovered over his shoulder. I let him pull me to my feet, smiling sheepishly at the lady.

"Do you have something in mind?" I looked over at Nox, was this what he wanted. "No, I don't think she does," he answered for me.

"Perfect. Start browsing, we can just try some options on and work from there," she said before she disappeared into the back of the store. "What is the occasion?" she asked. I looked at Nox again, he had not given any indication there was any occasion. Nox shifted nervously, glancing at me.

"She doesn't know yet," he answered.

"Nothing crazy. I don't want anything bright or sparkly," I added.

"Let's just try some options and see what you like." We all split up in the maze of fabric looking for options. Everything was bright and colourful, sparkles and sequences, silky and layered. *Ugh.*

"Sage," Nox called over the racks he was at the back with the lady at the fitting room. I quickly snatched a couple nearby dresses, and skipped over to them. Both of them had dresses of all colours following out of their arms.

"I would like to see you in all of them if that is ok? Even if you don't like them," Nox said.

"When you have tried them all on, if you don't find one you like we can find something similar to the ones you do," the lady added as she piled all the dresses we had picked into the small mirrored booth. There was so much fabric. I started with the ones that Nox had picked, maybe he would get bored after those were done.

I slipped my legs into the pale yellow gown and pulled it up, slipping the thin straps over my shoulders. It felt like water against my skin. It reached just past my knees but you could still see the scars on my lower legs. I looked at the dress in the mirror, swinging it back and forth.

I stepped out of the dressing room to Nox's eager eyes, I pulled my arms up to my chest trying to cover up. I felt bare, unprotected. Nox stayed silent looking at me, taking time to take in the dress, then waiting looking right at me. *What? No comment.*

"What do you think?" I asked.

"How do you feel?" he asked. *What did it matter?*

"I...feel uncomfortable," I answered.

"Ok. Next one?" he asked.

"What do you think?" I wanted to know what he thought. "Stunning." He had a fire in his eyes burning through the fabric of the dress going right to my skin. I flushed at his gaze. *Holy.* As I pulled the dress off, in the little booth, I glanced at the price tag. *What?* Seventeen hundred dollars? "Nox?" I called.

"These are expensive," I called out the changing room.

"Don't worry about it. It's my treat," he called back. *But it's so much.* It continued like this, I showed Nox each dress.

A blue one. One with fluffy sleeves. A pink one. One with a thousand layers. A green one. One with shining jewels. An orange one. A glittery one. A light brown one. A short one. A white one. A long one. A dark blue one. One that was nearly see-through. A silver one. A shimmery one. A tan one. One with lace. A gold one. One with fabric like water. A red one. One with holes in it. A lilac one. One with stripes. A black one. One with a scratchy bodice. A sage one. One with sleeves that reach the floor. A peach one. One with diamond straps. A teal one. One with gold seams. A gray one. One with a million beads on it. A falu one. One with no sleeves at all. A buttermilk one. One with large shoulders that stood up by themselves. A sand one. One that looked like a bathrobe. A walnut one. *So many dresses.*

None of them felt right. I felt bad, so many dresses and so much time wasted. I sat on the floor waiting as the shop lady pulled some more dresses based off of the elements I liked of the other dresses. "Why are we doing this?" I asked Nox.

"The pack has a dance. It's super important." Nox wrapped his arm around my shoulder, kissing my head. "I should have told you. I need you there," He whispered the last part into my hair. "Ok," I mumbled.

"Will you be my date?" he asked.

"Yes." The smile that graced his face was glowing with gratitude. I reached up and placed my hand on his cheek, he closed his eyes, the muscles in his face relaxing. The greatest gift he could give me. "I love you," I hummed.

"I love you too," he replied. The shop lady appeared, I stomped down the dread at another barrage of dresses to come. "Shoo." She waved her hands at Nox, who gave her a disgruntled look, but ultimately folded. "I found the dress." She pulled a dress bag from behind her back, handing it to me. I pulled the heavy curtain across the opening before pulling the dress out.

It was colourful. I slipped into the light fabric. The small slip was pale lavender, then over top of that was a single layer of a netted light fabric, it was soft. The slip was small, it had a sweetheart neckline with no straps, and stopped just above my knee. The fabric on top started at the collarbone and down my arms in loose sleeves. It started as the same pale lavender, then turned to pink -then darkened and turned to dark blue at the floor. It flared out in what the lady had claimed as an A-line skirt.

It was beautiful, little butterflies and sprigs of trees dotted the skirt, it was light, but covered my body. "Sage?" Nox was worried I was taking a long time looking at the dress. I stepped out watching his reaction. He smiled, but he had reacted positively to every dress. "How do you feel?" He had asked it before making any comments on all the dresses.

"Pretty." I bite my lip waiting to see if he would say anything else. "You are stunning. You look so happy." He had barely looked at the dress, I blushed deeply.

"So?" The lady asked, smiling. "I really like this one." I pulled at the skirt, running it through my fingers nervously. Nox walked over and picked me up, hauling me over his shoulder. He placed me back down in the dressing room spinning me around in my dress. "I will meet you at the front, I need to pay," he said, before leaving.

"Wait. What are you going to wear?" I asked him.

"I don't know yet. I was waiting till you found your dress so I could match." He kissed my head spinning me one more time before disappearing back into the store. I slipped back into my clothes and slid the dress back in the bag.

Sage

I am so tired of fighting. Each day is harder and easier at the same time. Each day I get a little stronger, I can do more, but each day the shadows in the back of my mind get darker and it takes so much more to fight them and I am losing slowly.

My dreams were haunted by the ghostly forest, no matter how much I walked, I ended back in the same clearing.

~

I walked down the hallway of our house. *Our house.* It was lined with bookshelves, they were stuffed to the brim with hundreds of different coloured books. Lots of brown and black leather, mixed with soft paper all colours of the rainbow. Each had a name printed on the spine. Reading each one as my finger reached it. All of the leather ones had dates as titles.

I gently eased one off the shelf, dated over a year ago. I flipped to the first page, it was a journal. It was Nox's. I slide it back on the shelf feeling self conscious about snooping through his personal thoughts. Moving on down the hall. A worn black book on the top shelf caught my eye. It had no title.

I pulled it off the shelf. The leather was worn and creased, it was larger than most books. I pulled the fraying cord from around its pages. Flipping it open. It was a sketchbook. I froze. The art. The first page was a concrete wall, with deep rivets carved into it, rust and blood coloured the wall. I knew this wall. I had stared at it for over two weeks. *It was my cell.*

How did...when...was he there? I flipped to another page turning away from that hateful memory. My world had become small and dark again. Nothing outside of the shadows dancing in my mind. The next page was my wrists, black and blue, with the cuffs digging so deeply into my skin that it cried red tears down to my elbows. I quickly flipped through each page, each one depicted a nightmarish memory I had buried deep in me. *What is this?*

A deeply twisted part of me whispered a darkly hateful thing. *Did he enjoy looking at this?* The last page at the back was a black and white painting. It was a dead forest, it stirred something in my mind, the ghostly trees seemed to scream at me.

"Sage?" I jumped out of my skin, snapping the book shut and tucking it behind my back as I turned to face him. "Yes?" I squeaked.

"You didn't respond," Nox responded.

"I'm sorry," I whispered.

"Are you ok?" he asked me.

"I…" I shifted, not sure how to answer. *How much did I really know about him? What did he keep from me?* He is an Alpha. *Of course he enjoys these … all Alphas are like this…* He shifted trying to peek behind me at the book. He slowly leaned over prying the book from my small hands. *Oh no.* "You found this…." He whispered looking down at the book. He looked pained. "What…" I started. "It's my journal." I waited.

"… my nightmares…" *Nightmares?* I reached out and placed my hand on his cheek. "I'm sorry. If they scared you, I know they are…. terrifying," He nuzzled into my hand, his voice thick with pain. "They are not nightmares," I mumbled. He did not respond to this.

"They are my memories…" I admitted. His gaze jerked up to me, his eyes shining yellow. He pulled me to his body, nuzzling my neck, his hot tears sliding over my skin. "I have heard of mates seeing each other in dreams but I never thought…" he mumbled.

"I'm here now. I am safe now," I promised.

"Mate," he pleaded.

Sage

That night I slept cradled between Nox's legs, wrapped in his arms. Though most nights I slept in his arms the feel of this night was drastically different.

~

By the morning Nox had calmed down enough to head to his office at the pack house. I had spent the morning reading on the couch, I was working my way through Nox's journals. I tucked the journal under my arm, questions floating around my head. *I could just go ask him.* It took some time for me to make my way to the pack house on foot. I missed being able to shift and run free, the wild wind in your fur. *Not that I got that for very long.* I had lost my wolf so soon after getting my other half.

My muscles ached as I climbed up the steps pushing the door open with my shoulder. I walked slowly down the hall, my eyes slowly adjusting to the difference in light. I hit something solid, bouncing back. "I'm sorry," I begged. I kept my eyes on their feet. "No worries," they said. I recognized that voice. *Nox's mother.* "You are Nox's mother," I state. I looked up to her face, she had his eyes and the same smile. "I am," she commented.

"You are Sage?" I nodded trying to smile at her. "Do you have a moment to chat?" she asked.

"Yes," I mumbled.

"Great!" She did not make any move to relocate. I stood my ground, lowering my gaze a little. Looking at her shoulders. "Do you plan on being Luna, and why?" She looked at me waiting. *Why do I want this?* "I want to support Nox. He carries too much weight," I answered finally.

"What if the pack does not accept you?" she continued.

" I… had not thought about that.." I looked at the floor. They could reject me. *They probably will.* "You don't have to be Luna, they can still love you as his mate and not as their Luna," she pointed out.

"I want to help Nox. Even if they hate me for it," I replied.

"They just might love you for it," she snipped. She walked off without another word. I lent against the wall waiting for my vision to clear.

~

I made my way, slowly, to Nox's office. The encounter with his mother rattled me, I could not take much more. I made it to the door of his office feeling stronger. I stepped up to the door, reaching for the door knob. "You can't just go in." I froze.

"The Alpha is busy. Don't ever waste his time with your useless bullshit. Don't even think about talking to him," the man growled as he grabbed my shoulders, pinning me to the wall. The world stopped, there was nothing but this large male and the wall to my back. "Get your hands off of her," I barely recognized the snarl, the body in front of me was ripped away from me. Air rushed back into my lungs. "Get out of my sight," he snarled at the man. He now stood in front of me, his chest a wall blocking me, protecting me. *Nox.*

"Alpha. This..this .. bottom of the pack...was disrespecting you.." he stumbled. "How?" Nox asked. Did he really think I would? *I would ever.* "She was just going to walk into your office," he announced.

"She is allowed to," Nox responded. The man stuttered and spluttered at Nox. "You. You have disrespected her. She is my mate," Nox growled at the now trembling man. "Pull a stunt like this again, and you are done in this pack." Nox turned around to face me, the cold mask of an Alpha watching me, his yellow eyes stone cold. Slowly it melted away to the loving gaze of the man I knew. He took a deep breath. "I need to hold you," he said quietly. I stepped into his waiting arms, his arms holding me close, his frame shaking against me.

"I am ok." Nox pulled me into the safety of his office. "But what he did was not," he snarled. I looked up expecting to be greeted by his yellow eyes, but the sparkle of his blue eyes met me. I gently ran my fingers along his brow, down his cheek, then along his jaw. The gentle growl emanates from his chest, soft and low, like a purr. *Happy.*

Nox's desk was still covered in maps, the maps overlapping. I pulled at the maps laying them on top of each other, upside down, slowly twisting the lower one and then the top one. "Sage?" Nox's hand hovered on my elbow. "It's… from my dreams," I whispered. I ran my fingers over the layer maps, it was a deep thick forest, one map had the stream running through the forest, the other had the clearing, one had neither. Only with all of them overlapping, could you see the final picture. *The clearing from my dreams.*

"He's here." I had no basis for my certainty, but I was. Nox looked at me, thinking -waiting- weighting the information. "Ok." He walked over and looked at the map. *Would he trust me? What if he didn't?* I was to stand by his side, but what if it means nothing? "I will be right back." He kissed my forehead, squeezing my shoulder before running from the room. I waited for him to return. He had left the door open, passersby looked in curiously, taken aback seeing me alone in his office.

"Saaggggggeeeeee!" Jake strolled in, no one batted an eye at him just walking in, but he has been the pack's Third for years. *They all know he belongs here.* "Nox just left," I commented.

"Yeah. I ran into him on my way up here." Jake chuckled at the memory. "Can I help you with anything?" Jake just smiled at me, his hair was tousled as if he had run his fingers through his hair many times. I did not respond. "Nox said to meet here." *Oh.*

"You ran out of there like your ass was on fire," Seth chuckled, leaning against the door, "was I that bad?"

"Nox wanted me here," Jake muttered.

"That doesn't answer my question." Seth did not move, staring at his mate. *He was really asking?* I should not be witnessing this. I shifted, knocking my toe into Nox's desk, trying to alert them to my presence. Jake smirked at his mate. *Oh the arrogance in that face.* "Well you are no me…." Jake walked closer to his mate slowly, " but…"

"Jake," Seth growled his name, rumbling deep in his chest, so much meaning underneath that one word. "You bring me unholy pleasure," Jake spoke against Seth's skin. Did they not care that I was here? *Clearly not.* "This is in fact my office," Nox snickered as he slipped past the two smirking at them. Was this what everyone else felt when Nox and I got distracted by each other?

"This meeting will go off the rails if you two fuck on my desk in the middle of it." Nox sat down at said desk, smiling at the blush that blossomed on my skin. "You did interrupt our fun with this meeting so it's only fair…" Seth ran his fingers through Jake's hair, *oh maybe it wasn't Jake who messed up his hair.* "Your mate is definitely not used to wolf society," Jake snickered at me.

"We are not shy about our love for our mate." Seth pulled Jake closer to him by his hips. *Oh Goddess they weren't really going to...* "Alright people, we have a meeting." James walked in the door putting an end to the conversation.

~

"How are you?" Nox sat back in his chair, watching me. This large Alpha, who bled power into the air in every movement cared for me, treated me like I was the moon and the stars, and the night in between. *How am I?* I was stressed, overwhelmed, tired, and…"Hungry." Nox gently pulled on my wrist, asking me to join him on the chair. I settled into his lap, sliding my hips along his leg, before settling on his hips. "What would you like to eat?" His hands settled on the tops of my hips, squeezing lightly. I sucked in a breath, his eyes roamed down my body as he bit his lip. I had a feeling what he had in mind was not food. I could feel what he had in mind under my thigh.

"Pie. Apple pie?" I asked quietly. "Done," Nox agreed. He smiled at me, shifting underneath me. His cock rubbing down the inside of my thigh. "Can I request something to eat?" *Oh, this man.* He lit a fire in my blood, it burned along every inch he touched me, pooling deep in my core. I squirmed under his gaze, lust danced in his eyes. "You." *Fuck.*

Nox

My damn mate. She was trouble. I could not pry my eyes from her swaying hips as we walked home to make her food. I shifted trying to pull the pinching fabric from my cock as I walked, only caring about the restriction of my pants and not whether people saw.

Not that my pack would care but let them judge me for finding my mate attractive. I love her. *Fuck. Her ass.* She was in so much trouble. Once we reached home, I did not bring her to our bed, like I wanted, but to the kitchen to make pie.

Getting her the food she wanted was more important than taking her to bed and showing her just how much she meant to me. "Beautiful. Can you grab a can of pie filling?" She nodded before digging through one of the cupboards looking for the apple pie filling. It didn't take long to whip up a pie for my mate, and now I get to express my love for her while we wait for it to bake.

Where did she go? I glanced round the room, panic digging its claws into me. *Sage?* No. No. Where is she? "Sage?" I called.

"Here." I ran around the corner to see her curled up on the floor. "What's wrong?" I fused over her hair trying to get her to look up at me. "Hurts," she whimpered.

"What hurts?" I questioned.

"Stomach." I rubbed her back in slow circles. *"Doc. Sage isn't feeling well."* I linked the doctor. Sage bolted up and ran out the room. Darting after her, I found her curled over the toilet. I rubbed her back sitting down next to her. She rocked back on her heels, before curling up on my legs. "Hugging you makes me feel better." Her arms wrapped around my waist. I ran my hand over her forehead, she had a slight fever, little trembles shook her body.

"I feel better. I don't want to go to the doctor," Sage whispered.

"Sage," I countered.

"No, I feel fine now," she insisted.

"Ok." I kissed her forehead, she did feel less feverish. "I like this."

"I love you." Such pale words for what I felt for her. "I love you too," she hummed. *Goddess-be-damned.* My mate was everything. *"Alpha. We found him."* I was linked.

Sage

After a night entwined in Nox's arms I felt like myself again, not a hint of pain or discomfort. I ran my hand over his chest, and down his waist, exploring his skin. The muscles that carved his figure, each mapped with scars. I ran my fingers slowly over his hip, tracing the three thick scars carved deep into his skin. Claw marks. "Enjoying the view?" I jumped looking up at his sleepy eyes. "Very much." I blushed as his eyes roamed my body, taking in each soft curve of my body.

"You are so beautiful," he rumbled. His eyes were no longer on my body, they were looking right at me, deep into my soul. "Stunning," he murmured. I leaned down pressing my lips to his hot skin, trailing down this chest, inch by inch. A low growl left his lips, growing deeper and as I got lower and lower. "Sage," he growled between his teeth.

"Sage you are stunning," he moaned. I ran my tongue over the soft white scars on his hip. "Fuck!" His fingers found my hair, gripping tightly. Having this big, strong, scarred Alpha relinquishing himself over to me was a power trip. I nipped at his skin above his hip, above his scars. "Sage." I loved how he growled my name. He growled at me, hooking his arm under my leg pulling me up his body. "You are temptation incarnate," he moaned.

"You aren't falling for it," I goaded.

"Are you ready?" He asked, and was deadly still, watching me, analyzing everything I did. "I..." I started. I don't know. I think I am, I want to be. I want him. He waited, watching me. "I trust you," I whispered and waited, watching him. "Okay." He took a deep breath, through his nose. A wicked smile blooming on his face. *Oh no.* He laughed a full, head thrown back, body shaking laugh.

"You smell amazing," He hummed as he ran a hand down my jaw, sliding down my neck pulling me close. "Your arousal..." his words petered off into a growl. "This is what I want," I whispered.

"Say it. I need you to say it," he edged. I had opened a dam in him, releasing him from his control. "I want to mate," I confirmed.

"Try again." The wicked smile he gave me before casting a blazing trail of kisses down my neck. "I want you to fuck me," I whined.

"That's better." His teeth nipped at my skin on my shoulder. "First..." He drawled, licking his tongue over my shoulder. "Food." *What? Why?* "No. Now," I grit, tugging at his hair. The growl it elicited from him was heavenly. "You will need your energy. I have so many plans," Nox promised.

"Like what?" I asked.

"You kept me waiting so long… We are going to do everything." I leaned back, bringing my back off the bed, pressing my body to his. The heat of his body seeped into my skin. My breast tightened, nipples budding, against his body. "Why wait," I begged.

"So we can do everything. We will need energy," Nox pressed.

"But…" I complained.

"I know you want my cock. Soon Beautiful. Trust me, I won't make you wait much longer," he promised.

"Please," I moaned as I rolled my hips up against him.

"You are testing my will with that begging," Nox groaned.

~

"What do you want to eat?" Nox asked.

"Waffles?" I suggested

"Ok." He started to putter around the kitchen.

"Can we skip the food and just go upstairs….?" I asked.

"I know you don't want to wait, but food first," Nox pressed. *Mean.* I wanted him. *Needed him.* His body. His soul. Mine. "Nox," I whined. He smirked at me, he pulled his shirt slowly off over his head, revealing his muscled chest. *Oh I could just lick every inch of him.* "Begging won't get you anywhere," Nox smirked.

"Nox!" I shrieked. *This was not fair!*

"Sage," Nox warned. *Oh Holy hell.* My eyes roamed up and down his exposed skin drinking him in. My whole body burned with my desire for him, slowly untied my waist band looking at him as I slowly inched the fabric over my ass. "Fuck!" he growled, his eyes darkening, before lighting on fire. He turned away from me. *No!* "Sage. Please." The muscles in his back were twitching as he slowly went about making waffles. "Sorry." I placed my hand on his back, the muscles under it tighten and then relaxed.

"I'm scared," he admitted. *What?* My mate, the fearless Alpha, was scared? "What of?" I asked.

"That you aren't ready. That I will hurt you," he confessed.

"You won't," I promised.

"Are you sure you know what you are agreeing to?" he asked. He still faced away from me, the waffle batter sitting untouched in front of him. "No. But I want this. I want you. I want us." He turned to face me, his face pinched in a frown, concern etched into every muscle. "Sage." Hearing my name on his lips was heaven and hell at the same time. So right, but oh so wrong too.

"Do you not want this with me?" I asked. Pain flashed through his eyes. He did not answer, he just watched his eyes darting over my face. His hands drifted down my back, electric sparks dancing in the wake of his fingers, then over my hips and on to my ass. His fingers gently dug into skin, hooking under my hips, he lifted me up into his arms.

"I have wanted this for as long as I can remember. I have wanted this with you since day one, I just wasn't sure you would get here. This gift, our love, is heaven. You are my other half, holding back my love for you has been my greatest strength and weakness. I don't want you to ever doubt my want, my need, for you," Nox whispered.

"Let me give you this gift," I whispered into his skin. His warm breath fanned over me, I could feel his smile as he pressed his lips to my shoulder over and over again. "My pleasure." He loosened his grip on my hips, I slid down his body a couple of inches. My hips lined up with his, I felt every inch of his desire for me, pressing into my wet, needy, desire for him.

"Food. First," he chided. His hands tightened on my ass pulling my hips closer to him, gasping as each little shift of his body ground his cock against me. "Nox," I breathed, willing, hoping, it didn't sound as much like a breathless moan to his ears as it did mine.

"Sage," he replied.

"By the Goddess," Nox groaned as he dragged his teeth over my skin, nuzzling my neck. "Stop!" I pushed against his chest, he backed up a couple steps. He was frozen, in place his mouth open, hands raised slightly. "I'm not ready," I stumble trying to rush the words out. *Not yet.* I'm not ready to be marked. *Mated, yes. Marked, no.*

"Ok." He backed up a couple steps to the stove, dropping his hands to his side. "Still want waffles?" he asked stiffly. He was moving slowly, talking quietly. He was worried about me, trying not to spook me, trying to keep me safe. *From him.* He didn't need to worry, I am always safe with him.

"Yes. I still want all of it. Just not marking. Not yet," I pleaded. He stilled. "I wasn't going to. We haven't had that conversation yet," he reassured. *He would always wait till I was ready.* My mate. "But you aren't ready right now. So Waffles, then we talk about if we still want to mate," he said.

"I want to mate," I confirmed. I wrinkled my nose at him baring my teeth.

"Horny much?" he teased.

"I want you. I want to mate with you. You are my mate, I want all of what that means," I counter.

"Waffles." *What?* Nox handed me a plate of warm waffles, dripping with syrup. He sat down next to me at the table with his own heaping plate. He wolfed them down in record time. I picked my way through the plate, but it disappeared too quickly for my liking. I spooned the last mouthful, dripping with syrup, savoring the taste.

"Beautiful," Nox hummed as he smiled at me, pulling me close. He leaned down looking at me, like I was the moon and the stars, and everything in between. The wicked smile was all the warning I got before he licked me, his tongue dancing over my lips. He trailed a couple kisses along my jaw. "Delicious," he muttered, adding a devilish little flick of his tongue behind my ear. *Oh Nox!* My man would be the death of me. "Now that you have eaten. Shall I take you to our bed?" he teased.

Sage

I picked at the threads on the bed. *What's taking so long?* I tugged the fluffy blanket tighter around my shoulders. "Nox?" I called.

"Right here." Nox swaggered back into the room. "I thought we were going to…" I trailed off -my skin heating. "We are. Don't worry. But I am Alpha of this pack, just tying up some loose ends so we don't get interrupted." He closed the bedroom door behind him. I let go of the blanket, it dropped to our bed.

He stilled, looking at me, his eyes not moving from mine. In one moment he was still -in the next he was gliding across the room his hand outstretched. He crawled across the bed. His hand sliding over my ribs, pulling me flush to his body. "Stunning," he whispered, pulling my hair off of my back. His breath fanned out over my skin.

"Though I was looking forward to unwrapping you, this is just as good," he groaned. He slid his other hand down over my hip, cupping my ass. His fingers tightened on my ass as he kissed my neck -nipping at my shoulder.

His fingers inched lower down my thigh, he hooked his fingers under my knee, he pulled gently, shifting my weight over to my other hip. His hand on my hips looped round, flat against my spine. "Do you trust me?" he asked.

"Yes." His grip on my knee tightened a little, he pulled my leg up and around his hip. Shifting my weight onto his arm, pulling me up into his arms. Pulling me close he spun around, sitting back down on the bed my weight pressing me into his hips. I shifted pulling my weight off of his boner. "Stop moving like that," he moaned.

"I *want* you on my cock," Nox growled.

"I don't want to hurt you," I whispered. Nox laughed, not a sound left his lips, but I could feel it under my hand, in his chest. "You won't," he promised. I rolled my hips back, leaning into him. His lips met mine, his sneaky tongue darting out licking at my bottom lip. I smiled against his lips. *Do it.* I parted my lips, before he could react I gently closed my mouth over his lip, nipping at his bottom lip. The low growl it pulled from him was electric. His hands gently moved over my skin, down my ribs over my hips, along my thighs. His fingers tracing invisible designs over my skin.

"Mate," he whispered as my fingers snagged in his waistband.

"Mate," I echoed as I fisted his shirt. He gently pulled my fingers from the fabric, before pulling it off over his head. He tossed it aside as I ran my hands over his muscled chest, peppering little kisses over his scars.

"Will you tell me the stories of these?" I ran my fingers lightly over an angry puckered section of skin. "Later," his voice was painful and gruff. I flattened my hand to his chest, feeling his heat sink into my skin. His heart beat hammered under my touch, I gently curled my fingers into his muscle. The low chuckle it pulled from Nox's lips, was like darkness and spice, gently caressing my skin.

"What? Do you want to be in control?" His smirk promised of all the wicked things he would let me do to him. To have that power over him. *An Alpha.*

"You can be if you want… but I think right now you want to be shown just how much I want you," Nox breathed. His hand joined mine, tightening my grip on him. He slipped his fingers into my hair, his palm resting on the back of neck. His grip tightened on my neck, carefully avoiding putting too much pressure on my spine.

His teeth grazed my shoulder, sending shivers down my spine, he walked up my neck with little nips and kisses. "I can smell your arousal," he growled in my ear.

"I can feel yours," I giggled. I shifted forward a little, rubbing my arousal against him. His hands flew to my hips, pulling me closer to him, growling, as he gently bit down on my shoulder. A gasp let my lips, his teeth on my skin, is cock rubbing against me. "Your pants," I warned.

"I want you to soak them through," Nox groaned. He pulled once again pulling my body along his arousal. Oh I could feel every glorious inch of his cock through his pants. His fingers blazed trailed up my body as they roamed up my hips, over my stomach, and slowed to a stop at my ribs. The back of one of his fingers, brushed, feather light against the underside of my breast. Goosebumps scattered across my skin at his light touch, my nipple pebbled, feeling tight and pinched.

My breast ached and felt heavy on my chest, craving more of his curious fingers. Nox let out a low chuckle, as his finger traced circles around my nipple, pulling small gasps from my lips. Nox lifted his finger from my skin, I groaned at the absence of him.

He smirked at me as he slowly licked his finger, not breaking eye contact. He gently paced the now wet finger back on my nipple, the cold shock rippling through every nerve in my body. "Good?" he checked.

"Very," I moaned.

"Good," Nox growled. Nox dipped his head, towards my collar, kissing my shoulder, as an arm snaked around my lower back, he lifted me up slightly dipping his lips even lower. They brushed the top of my breast lightly, the deep tugging in my breast tightened at his touch. He nipped lightly at the skin just above my nipple, before he ran his tongue over the sensitive bud. His hand skimmed over my other breast, cupping it lightly as his tongue ran little circles around my nipple. I shifted, sliding my hips against his cock, trying to inch closer to his touch. His breath fanned out over my skin as he chuckled into my chest.

His hand left my breast, missing his warmth, I reached out grabbing his hand to bring it back.

"Trust me," he begged. He gently pulled his hand from my grip, sliding his hand over my hip and cupping my ass. Lightly squeezing, digging his fingers into my muscles. He placed a gentle kiss to my lips before pulling me closer, along his cock. His fingers danced lightly over my hips, as I rolled them against him. A low hum bubbled up from his chest as his grip on my ass tightened.

"Sage." He lifted my hips up off of him, I whined at him. "Sage, you need to trust me. Trust that if I stop doing something you like, it won't be for long," he chuckled. I nuzzled my nose into the side of his face. His fingers drifted down my thighs.

"Now. Stay there for a moment," he commanded. His hands left my body, I missed his warmth. I reached out and placed my hand on his neck. His hands tugged at his pants, pulling them off, wrapping his arms around my legs to tug them out from under us.

He gently pressed both his palms against my hips, his hands warming the sensitive flesh, bringing me back down to the top of his thighs. My tongue ran over my lips as I looked at him, his eyes tracking my movement. I shifted forward a little, his cock brushing up against my inner thigh.

"Please," I begged. Nox paused, completely still, before exploding into action. His arms held me in place as he lifted me up as he rose from the bed, spinning us around. Dropping me smoothly to the bed, my back bouncing a little against the soft mattress. His knee inched my legs open a little more, spreading me out before him. His eyes burned over my skin taking me in −a buffet for his pleasure. "As you wish," he hummed. He leaned forward, resting his weight on his arms, just under my arms.

"Relax," he whispered as his head brushed my slick arousal. Nox nipped gently at my shoulder, licking up my neck. Slowly, he eased himself to me till he was sitting right at my entrance. The head of his cock nudged against the entrance of my pussy -pressing gently into me. He slowly pressed deeper, sliding his girth into me. My muscles tightened against him, fighting him.

I gasped, slamming my hand into his chest, he stopped. "You okay?" Panic flashing through his eyes, I nodded as I gulped down some air. "Continue," I begged. He kissed my shoulder, before continuing to ease each glorious inch of him in me. After a few moments his hips rested against my thighs as I took the full length of him in me.

"Control," Nox ground out to himself, I ran a gentle hand down his back, every muscle in his body was so tense. He growled at my touch, biting into my shoulder.

"Don't worry about it," I whisper to him, as I gently pull myself off him slowly. His hands grip the sheets -as he takes me slowly and starts to thrust deeper. Slowly - millimetre at a time, letting my body adjust to him. I rested my hand on his back. "Nox," I begged. He sank deep into my pussy at his name, a moan escaping my lips.

"Let go of the control," I commanded. He paused.

"Sage." My name was heaven in that sex drugged, lust filled voice of his. Slowly he picked up speed, sinking deeper into my core each time. The muscles in his back relaxed and flexed with his movement, the tension leaving his body.

The world began to melt away, leaving just our bodies, our breath and moans, and nothing else. Nox's hand snaked under my shoulder blade, lifting me up slightly as he gripped on to me, stopping me from inching away with each thrust.

My fingers dug into his skin as pleasure snaked and pooled in my hips. Anticipation wound through my muscles as pleasure sparked through my brain. Pleasure built higher and higher, as I felt the full extent of just how powerful Nox's body was.

"Nox." I had stopped paying attention to all the sounds Nox had me making, moaning, gasping, whimpering, begging, screaming in pleasure. I could not take much more the pleasure spiked though my brain, a dam about to burst.

"Sage. Relax. Let yourself feel good," he gritted out, each word punctuated with a particularly well placed thrust. The world stopped. The dam broke.

All my muscles tensed, then relaxed, as the orgasm rocked my body. The only thing I sensed outside of the roaring pleasure sweeping through my body, was Nox saying my name.

Slowly my mind swam back to my body. We were both panting, Nox rested his body against mine, keeping the majority of his weight on his elbows. "Nox," I whispered.

"Sage." Nox slowly lifted his body from mine, rolling to the side, flopping to the bed. Gently he tugged me close to him, wrapping me tightly in his arms. "Next time, I want to taste your orgasm," Nox vowed. I blushed at the image of him with his tongue between my legs. Especially now, as I was a sticky mess.

"Okay," I whispered before sleep clouded my brain.

~

We slept for a couple hours, before I was pulled from sleep by my stomach demanding food.

"We should get cleaned up first," he suggested. Nox gently took both my hands in his, guiding me to the bathroom. We hopped in under the warm stream of water together. I reached for some soap - my fingers brushed the top of the slick soap -to start cleaning up the once sticky, now dried mess on my legs.

"No. Let me," he instructed. Nox pulled the soap from my hands, quickly kissing my forehead before kneeling down to clean me. I watched as he rubbed the soap to get the suds going and gently ran his hands over my legs, taking the time to make sure I was completely clean. Once he was satisfied with my legs he moved on to my hips, then my stomach, back, and arms. He kissed me as he gently worked some shampoo into my hair. Carefully helping me wash out the shampoo to make sure none got in my eyes. He gently rubbed my cleanser on my face, kissing my face once he washed it off.

"My Sage," he worshiped.

"My Nox," I hummed in prayer.

Nox

"Nox?" Jake linked. *"Yes?"* I replied.

"We need to talk face to face." That sounded bad.

"I will meet you in my office in half an hour," I noted. I wrapped my arms around Sage taking in the feeling of her in my arms, her scent, her weight, what it felt like to have her soul near me. "Sage." I curled a strand of her hair around my finger. She hummed noncommittally not looking up at me.

"I have to go to the office," I informed her.

"What? No!" Her head snapped up staring at me. "I won't be long," I promised.

"Ok," she grumbled.

"Can I go for a walk?" she asked.

"You can do anything," I encouraged. I rubbed my nose along her neck, kissing her where one day my mark will sit on her skin. *One day, till then I will take everything she gives me.* "Be careful. Don't go far," I reminded her.

"Come back soon." She smiled at me, kissing my cheek, before bouncing off the couch to get her shoes. I pulled her into a tight hug, as she reentered the room, memorizing every atom of her being.

"When we are back.. Can we…." She trailed off as she tugged at her shirt, covering her face. I pulled her shirt off her face, lifting her chin till she was looking at me. "…last night." Her face flushed as she averted her eyes looking down. "Yes," I replied. I tilted her chin up just a little more as I captured her mouth in mine. A promise, a taste of what was to come tonight.

"You are so cute when you blush. Don't ever worry about asking for sex. If I had my way we'd never leave the bedroom," I asserted. Her flush deepened as I whispered my words against her lips. I took one last deep breath of her scent, it had changed, now her scent was laced with her arousal.

I ducked out the door before I could blow off Jake. Jake stood in my office, stiff and muscles tense, arms crossed over his chest. *Shit.* "We have a major problem," he grunted.

"A security breach," James pipped in. They looked at each other, James crossed his arms over his chest mirroring Jake. "A member of the pack has been threatened," Jake noted.

"How?" I demanded. Jake held up a couple sheets of paper, the loopy chicken scratch hard to make out from this distance.

"This needs to be handled carefully." I glared at him. *Like I don't know what's at stake.* "Where is Sage?" James asked slowly. "What. She's safe. I was just at home with her," I answered.

"Sage is the one being threatened." *She just went on a walk.... I* bolted out the room. *SAGE!* She wasn't home, but then she had just left for a walk. My bones and muscles ached as I started to shift, eating up ground as fast as I could to reach her. I circled the house once, twice, and then a third time before I picked up her scent.

I dodge through the trees, following her scent, deeper and deeper into the woods. The world blurred around me, the feeling in my paws gone, nothing registered as I ate up land. *How did she get so deep in these woods so fast? Sage! Please! COME ON!*

I was coming up to the old fishing cabin, my paws sinking into the loose mud. Digging my claws into the mud -fighting to keep my balance as I rounded the corner to the edge of the lake. My eyes searched the lake taking in the rotten planks, broken glass, and plant infested cabin with it. The structure was falling into the brown sludgy water.

Sage stood knee deep in the water looking over the building in front of her. "Sage!" I shifted and ran over to her. Ignoring the squishing mud between my toes as I wade to her. Her head snapped back as I came up behind her.

"Nox?" Her brow crinkled as she looked at me. Her weight shifted from her left to right foot as her attention returned to the cabin. "Can we go in there?" she asked, pointing.

"No. It's falling apart and dangerous," I answered.

"That's sad," she pouted. Sage just kept watching the old building, a single tear falling slowly down her cheek. I slipped my finger into her palm, she didn't look back at me, but her fingers tightened on mine. "Let's get cleaned up," I suggested. Mud coated her legs all the way up over her knees and along her thighs. *How is she this gorgeous covered in mud?* Slowly she turned from the cabin towards me, her grip on my hand tightened as she looked at me. Quietly we both headed back towards home.

"I was worried about you," I whispered. We were over half way home before either of us spoke. "Why?" she wondered.

"I.." I paused. *Did she need to know this?*

"Someone threatened your safety, and I didn't know where you were," I answered.

"Who?" she asked, again.

"I don't know," I admitted. That hurt more than anything, I trusted I could keep her safe when she was with me, but not knowing who or when she was in danger? *She's just so small.*

~

"Nox," James sauntered up beside me. I had left Sage home alone in the bath. She was quite lost in her thoughts. I needed to look into this letter more, I had bolted in a panic before but I needed every piece of information I could get. "James," I greeted.

"You mated her," he stated. He didn't need to say anything more. I knew what he was implying. "Yes." I looked at him, not budging an inch. "Just be careful," he warned. He pulled ahead intent on walking away. "I am," I reassured.

"She's my Luna. Don't hurt her," he tossed over his shoulder before leaving me in the dust. I made it to my empty office, everything abandoned around the room.

I got down to studying the letter, recent reports, the maps, with each passing minute the pressure in my head turned to pounding then into a piercing headache. I rubbed at my eyes, and pressed at my forehead. I closed my eyes for one moment, a rushing whoosh as my head plummeted to meet the desk before me, my skull never met the table.

It was completely black -no wait- it wasn't all black. It was black, but something darker swirled through the black. Little dark lights started to spark and twinkle through the murk. *What was happening?* "Nox," a distant voice whispered. *Who was that?* "Hello?" I swung around searching the darkness looking for the voice. It came from all around me.

"Behind you." I whipped around to come face to face with unblinking creamy white eyes.

"Her life was not supposed to be like this. All of my children are born of my love, but once they make their way down from the stars their fates are out of my hands. Those who walk alone in the darkest parts of this world are reborn with my light," I heard her voice echoing around us but her lips did not move.

"Who are you?" I asked.

"Oh my child. You know who I am. You turn to me every time you need help," the voice echoed.

"I don't know who you are," I insisted.

"I am the Moon." *What?* "How many times have you come to me with your hopes and dreams?" they asked.

"And mistakes and worries. I listened to them all," she whispered. *Moon Goddess*

"Oh child." She seemed sad looking at me, her milky eyes swirling like smoke. She stood before me, if she took a step forward her hair would be brushing my nose, her hair was pure white no yellow to be seen or roots showing through.

"Goddess," I stumble, barely more than a whisper.

"Yes," she hummed.

"It's …It's an honour." I fight the urge to kneel before her.

"Don't!" She snapped curtly at me. "What?" I stepped back from her, my heel knocking into my other foot. "No honorifics," she insisted. I stilled. "I don't have much time," she continued.

"Sage," I entreated.

"The life she has lived is not the one she was meant to. She grew up in darkness. Alone. A wolf's soul is not meant to be away from my light. The darkness did not break her. I know things are tough right now, but it did not break her. She is a powerful wolf, and when her time in the physical world is over she will join me, but do not fret she will not join me for some time."

"I don't understand," I mumbled.

"I must go. You will in time. Love her, show her the light," she whispered, her voice echoing in the dark. Slowly her hair started to lift off her back, slowly she floated up off of the inky black floor, bright white light shining out from beneath her skin. I blinked to flush the tears welling up in my eyes.

I blinked a couple of times as my eyes adjusted to the warm yellow light. I lifted my head from my desk, running my arm across my face as the drool slid down my check. *What the fuck just happened??*

The world blurred as my head pounded. I crashed to the floor, bringing half my desk with me. "Nox!" A pair of hands wrenched at me. As they tugged at my body the movement sent waves of nausea over me, and my head spinning. "Nox!" Jake's blurry face swam into focus. "Nox!" Jake strained my head swimming as my back hit the desk, Jake's hands stilling holding me up. "What the hell? Are you ok?" he yelled.

"I don't know. I don't know," I stumbled over my tongue. I rubbed at my head the pounding pulse fading away. " I need Sage," I mumbled.

"I'll go get her. You ok for a minute?" Jake asked, standing up.

Nox

"What happened?" Sage came darting through my door and right to my side, her hands hovering over my arm, flitting around in the air as her eyes roamed over every inch of me. "I'm ok." I pulled her into a tight hug, breathing in her sweet scent. *I am too lucky to have her.* "I love you," she hummed.

"I love you too," I sighed and took Sage's hands in mine, bringing her up with me.

"Let's go home." I swept the loose strands of her wild hair out of her face, place a loving kiss on her forehead. "Are you sure you are okay?" She frowned at me, her forehead and eyes creasing. "Now that you are here I'm perfect." I ran one finger gentle over the crease on her forehead. She pulled away, running her hand over her face, shaking out her hair. "Home?" I asked.

"Yes," she sighed.

~

"You want to go on a date now?" I asked. *What is going on in this woman's mind?*

"Well..not a *date*..a walk." She fiddled with the cuff of her sweater. *A walk.*

"A walk," I repeated.

"Yes," she confirmed.

"I don't know about this," I groaned.

"Please." Sage pouted at me and my resolve faltered .. *It's just a walk ...*"It's dangerous. The pack is in danger. You are in danger," I explain.

"We won't leave the pack," she reassured.

"Ok, but I have one condition..." I started.

"Which is..." Sage stepped back and looked at me, her fidgeting stopped.

"It is a date," I offer.

"And we will go on more?" She asked smiling up at me shyly at her suggestion.

"As many as you want." I leaned over, slipping my hand into hers, pulling her close and breathing deeply. The smell of her hugging my brain. "Where shall we walk?" I asked.

"Let's just go and see where our feet take us?" Sage suggested.

"Ok," I hummed.

"I love you," Sage said.

"I love you too," I replied. Her small hands wandered their way up my shirt -her fingers wrapping around the neck of my shirt. Looking down at her small fingers turning white as she clung to the fabric. My hands met hers bringing them to my lips, and placed kisses over each digit, softer than a dove's wing, lighter than the first snow. *A ring would look so good on her finger.*

Sage ran around the house getting her shoes and a coat, her wild hair floating in crazy whisps.

~

We ambled along the edge of the woods weaving in and out of the dabbled trees, Sage's eyes swept over the trees taking in the symphony of greens dancing around us. With each wonder her eyes spotted her face light up, the way a dark green ivy traced designs up the pale bark of a tree and the grass was in fact not grass but a patchwork of wildflowers, pale purples and light blues, weaved with greens of every texture, broken up by yellows and reds.

I had walked these woods a thousand times and the beauty was lost on me, but watching her take it all in was seeing it for the first time again. I reached out slowly, my fingers running like water down her elbow to her wrist, settling in her palm. Her hand flexed lightly around mine before settling in my hand, our fingers weaving together.

It wasn't until we lapped our house for the third time did we slow down, the warm sunlight peeked through the leaves, the sun was dark orange and kissing the land.

Sage slipped her hand from mine, the chill evening air curling up in my once warm hand, missing the ghost of her touch.

She was already slipping inside our home. *How can everything be so perfect?* Swinging the door open again as I stepped through, an excited grin graced my Angel's face. Sage jumped at me, throwing herself into my arms. I held her up, bringing that beautiful smile level with me.

"Stunning." She made a small hum in disagreement. I spun her around, her head tilting back as a laugh bubbled up out of her. *Intoxicating. All of her is intoxicating.* Sage lifted her head to my shoulder, resting against me. Deep breaths of her sweet scent, slowly my lips traced her shoulder, and up her neck till I reached her hairline. The scent of her arousal started to over power every scent in my nose. I trailed little kisses along her jaw, starting at her ear.

"Addictive," I whispered into her skin. "Yes, you are," she whispered back. *Not what I meant.* "I meant you." I let my tongue dart out, sliding along Sage's bottom lip. An excited gasp left her at my touch. Encouraged by her reaction I continued, licking her top lip lightly. Her lips part, her eyes sparkling up at me. *By the Goddess she's beautiful.*

"Sage," I whispered.

"Nox," she echoed.

"Can I take you to our bed?" murmured into her skin. "Yes." The blush that bloomed in her cheeks and flooded down her neck was the prettiest shade of pink.

Sage

Nox wrapped his arms around me, lifting me off my feet -by only a couple inches. Spinning me around before heading towards the stairs to our room. One strong arm looped under my ass lifting me over his shoulder, my head bouncing around his mid-back. "Nox!" My fingers splayed across his back, the pads of my fingers curling around the soft fabric of his shirt. A small giggle escaped my lips as Nox bounded up the stairs.

With a quick flick of his arms I was flipped over his shoulder and bounced off the bed, I flung out my arms to catch myself. Slowly my eyes traveled up his body as he stood in front of me, at the end of the bed. My eyes locked on to him, looking up at him from my sprawled potion on the bed. "Beautiful," he whispered more to himself. I glanced down at my thighs and stomach. *I look so different now. Is it better?*

"Stunning," Nox whispered his lips trailing kiss over my hips, burning tingling impressions left behind his touch, then prickling coolness as air danced over my flushed skin. His warm tongue flicked out searing across my skin. Lifting his lips from my skin he gently blew cold air over my wet skin. His lips reconnected with my skin, trailing slowly up my stomach, giving each inch of my skin all the love and attention before moving up. The top tufted of his hair tickled against the bottom swell of my breasts. He paused right as his eyes leveled with the apex of my bosom.

He did not leave me waiting long, deftly his tongue darted out tracing the gap between my breasts. His careful touch pulled a sharp gasp from my lips, the warm air of his chuckle fan over my skin before he continued up my body. He peppered light kisses over my collarbone.

"How are you doing beautiful?" His words sounded a little breathy. *How am I doing?* "Good," I whispered hoping he would continue with his lips. "Use your big girl words," Nox purred.

"Please just continue, it feels amazing!" I plead just wanting to feel him on my skin. "As you wish." Gently he wrapped his hands around my wrists guiding them to his shoulders, placing them right at the base of his neck. His hands skimmed down the side of my body, skipping over my ribs. His grip danced on my hips, before pulling me up and on to his lap. After I had settled on him, he slid his hands down my thighs to my knees, pausing before he gently wrapped my legs around his waist.

"Nox," I whined.

"Sage." *Oh Goddess when he says my name like that.* I shifted my weight from one hip to the other, then back again.

"Ready beautiful?" *Am I?* "Yes." *I am.* The smile that graced my mate's face was wicked and burning, any worry I had vanished into smoke. "Good." His fingers flexed gently into my flesh. I gently hooked my ankles behind his back, bringing me that little bit closer to him, the peak of my breasts brushing up against him.

A small growl rumbled through his chest as my full weight settled on his cock. I started to move back as his arousal pressed against my inner thigh. "Don't" It almost sounded harsh but the look on his face was far from it. "You feel so good, and I bet you taste even better." My whole body heated up at his suggestion. I could only guess at what shade of red my face had become. It wasn't until my finger tips dug into his skin did I realize I had reached out for him.

"What? Do you like the idea of that?" He smirked at me, not breaking eye contact as his tongue darted out and skimmed over his lips. I could not pull my eyes away from him. I let out an embarrassing squeak instead of the words I had been trying to form. "What was that beautiful?" The smile gracing his face evidently knew what I meant and knew what he was doing to me. I just watched him for a moment before opting for nodding my head.

"Lay back." He gently guided my head to the pillow behind me, keeping my hips on his lap. I looked up at him from my odd angle, my head buried in my chest. Nox shifted back, sliding his arms under me keeping my hips elevated, gently taking my weight in his arms and not on my neck.

"Ready?" I only nodded watching his every movement from the pillows. He placed his hands on my thighs, slowly spreading them, as they parted cool air licks over my sensitive skin. My heart beat pounded in my pussy as he looked down at my center.

"You look delicious," he purred. His head dipped between my legs, my stomach flip flopped in anticipation. Nox's warm breath fanned out over me as he looked at me over my stomach, he was inches from touching me. He hovered over me, just watching my face as his lips were inches from my heated core. "You are so wet, and I have yet to touch you," he growled. *Is that good?*

"Am I?" I started to shift as my hand drifted over to myself to see what he was talking about. "Very. Your arousal is intoxicating," his voice deep with worship. His fingers flexed into my hips to stop my movement. The tips of my index finger brushed my sensitive flesh. A small twist of pleasure coursed through me at my touch. I pulled my fingers away from my flesh, it was warm and damp beneath my touch. I looked down at my fingers, they glinted and gleamed back at me, a shiny substance on the end.

Nox leaned over, his tongue darting out, licking my fingers clean. A groan came from him, as his tongue retreated back in his mouth, his eyes shutting.

"Divine," he murmured. When he reopened his eyes a wild energy seemed to swim in them, as if the control he was barely holding onto was released. Almost instantly his head dipped, his lips met me. My hands flung out and grabbed onto anything they could, the air in my lungs gone. The small taster of pleasure my own fingers had given me was nothing compared to the feeling of his lips brushing me.

"Nox," I breathed into the air –at the sound of his name, his tongue darted out and gave me a quick lick. I swear my vision went black as his tongue reached the top of my pussy. As his breath fanned out over the area he just licked, my vision came back.

"Again!" I gasped out my legs flexing out once to dispel a mild cramp starting in them. "Of course." This time he did not stop after one lick, he kept licking me over and over again slowly up from the bottom, each time stopping at my clit, swirling his tongue in small circles and giving it a light suck before lifting away from me and repeating it -again and again.

With each touch of his tongue my body bucked and jerked, a wide array of noises leaving my lips. "Sage," Nox purred into my flesh, my fingers released the bed and flew to his hair instead. A groan as my fingers pulled at his hair pulling him closer, not letting him pull his tongue from me. The movements of his tongue just got faster, and more impassioned. The muscle in my abdomen tightened and tightened as his pace increased. I tipped my head back, as things started to go fuzzy, my head sank into the fluffy pillow.

"Nox." I gasped. My breath stuck in my throat, his lips closed over my clit. The tightness in my core let go, pleasure soaring up my body wrapping around every part of my mind. My arched body hit the bed under me as all my muscles relaxed the echoes of pleasure still beating through me.

Nox lifted his head from between my thighs, the same liquid that he cleaned off of me earlier -ran down his chin now. His eyes were a light with desire and satisfaction. He shifted his weight forward on to his arms sliding one out from under me. His free hand went to his chin, wiping me off of him. He looked at his hand before sliding his fingers into his mouth —cleaning them off.

Why was this so attractive? Once Nox had licked every ounce of my orgasm off of himself he leaned forward placing his spare arm next to my hip, rolling his weight forward over his hips. Slowly he stalked up my body, his eyes locked with mine. "Ready for more?" *More?!? How could I possibly take more? Did I want more?*

"Yes," I begged. My voice sounded a lot more sure than I thought it would. Nox placed a kiss on the right side of my neck then my left. Then another one on my left cheek then mirrored on my right. Dipping his body down, his weight on his elbows, till it brushed up against every inch of mine –his lips brushed mine lightly before kissing me with the passion of a thousand nights.

"We stop any time you want. Just say so." His fingers traced small circles on my shoulder, mimicking his earlier movement of his tongue. "I was right, you taste amazing," Nox admitted. Searing heat flooded my veins —I must look like I've been burnt; yet the reverence that Nox was looking at me with did not fade. Gently his fingers grazed me, parting my aching pussy, my heart beat picked up –the matching pulse in my core picking up too.

A warm hard pressure kissed up against me, my eyes widened. *He's so big.* A sharp twinge went through me as his head started to stretch my walls. He froze, not even breathing. "Are you okay?" My body slowly relaxed around him –I nodded.

"Just go slow," I stuttered. He paused a heart beat or two before gently leaning his weight forward. Each millimetre his cock slid into me left an uncomfortable feeling in my abdomen for a couple of moments before my body adjusted. Using his body weight to slowly let me accumulate to his size, but without being jerky –without stopping and starting. "How are you feeling?" he asked as he slid his full length all the way in, his hips resting lightly on my inner thighs. I waited a moment till the dull ache was swiped away to the pleasure.

"Amazing," I sighed. Nox leaned in over me, kissing my shoulder lightly. Our bodies blended into one, becoming an action and a reaction, he moved, I moaned, and repeated. Our breathing sinked as the pleasure built up in me, tension pooling in my hips, snaking up my core. "Nox!" I cried out his name. His cock worked my arousal tighter, and tighter. I could feel the slick of my arousal dripping down my thigh, spreading over his hips as they made contact with me. My brain started to go fuzzy, as the pleasure caressed my mind, singing me into a daze.

My fingers curled gently into his hair, pulling lightly on the gossamer strands. "Sage," he begged. My name was more a plea than anything else. "Let go of control." My words echoed his of the other day, with a deep breath –he picked up speed. Nox curled his fingers into the fabric of the pillows beneath me.

"Sage!" He growled out my name, his head dipping down to rest on my shoulder, at the sound of my name, the dam broke in my mind. Pleasure sparked through every muscle in my body. I panted, my legs hooked over Nox's, my fingers still in his hair, neither of us moved.

Nox

Eventually, I had Sage wrapped in a blanket and downstairs for some food. I leaned down, looping my arms around her knees -lifting her just enough to set her on the counter. "So, what are we eating?" I placed one hand either side of her leaning in.

"I'm not hungry," she refused.

"We just burned a ton of energy. We need to refuel. You pick." I was not letting this go. She needed to eat after what we just did, I was starving. "Fruit," she answered. Of course she'd pick fruit, it was her go to safe food. *At least it's something.*

"Fruit it is," I confirmed. I turned and busied myself with preparing a wide variety on a large plate. As I set the plate on the counter next to Sage she grabbed the largest piece of mango from the plate and slid off the counter. I watched her carefully as she munched on the mango, sitting down on the floor right below where she sat. Once she finished her piece of mango she didn't grab another one.

"Another one," I encouraged. I reached over and offered her the plate. She shook her head. "Please," I begged. She shook her head again looking at the floor and not me. "I'm worried about your eating," I admitted.

"I'm worried about you!" She burst out finally looking up at me. "What?" I asked.

"I am *worried* about you!" She damn near yelled at me –I stood completely still. *What?!* It took a couple moments for my shock to wear off. "You have been so stressed lately," she defended. She had gone quiet and was looking back at the floor. Before I could form words in response I reached out, hooking my fingers lightly under her chin, raising her gaze to meet mine.

"N..." I start, the disappointment that flickered in her eyes hurt. I stopped, closing my eyes –letting out my breath slowly. "Yes. I am but I don't want you to worry," I soothed. I leaned over and pressed my lips to her forehead. With her cradled against me, her head resting against my lips, my hand snuck out and grabbed a strawberry off the plate. Leaning back just an inch, I offered her the plump fruit.

"Well I am and I want to be." She took a bite of the berry, taking only half. *It's a start. Wait what did she say??* "You want to worry about me?" I clarified.

"No... but I can tell you are stressed." She started to pick at the fruit left in the bowl, to distract herself. "I'm ok, don't worry about me," I reassured.

"But I'm your mate!" She dropped the fruit back in the bowl as she snapped at me, a tear sliding down her cheek as she glared at me. "Yes, you are," I agreed. I smiled softly at her, brushing the tears from her skin. "We are in this together!" *She had a point but to put this on her when she was so fragile and still healing I could not break her like this.* I waited, trying to find a way to explain why to her.

"Yes we are." *I have no reason but my own fear.* I blow out all the air in my lungs before continuing. "It's about the pack's safety," I admitted. I looked at her, I could practically see the gears in her mind working to digest what I was telling her.

"You are a good leader." *What? That had nothing to do with the pack's safety...right?* I couldn't think about how quickly she had cut through me to the core of my fear. *I couldn't think about that.* "What can I do to help?" she asked.

"Distract me," I whispered.

"How?" she asked.

"Guess," I purred.

"I don't know," she back peddled. She had barely thought about it, her brow pinched. "Guess," I repeated. I smiled at her. "Oh," she gasped. The crimson flush of her skin starting in her cheeks before spreading to the rest of her body, her gaze slowly racked up my body before settling on my eyes.

Her small hands run up my body, my muscles tensing under her touch trying not to give away just how much she affected me. As her hands reached my shoulders she had to stand on the tip of her toes to reach. Gently she pressed down, guiding me to sit on the counter. I watched as her fingers trailed down my body again, the blood thrummed as her fingers made it to my waist. "What are you gonna do?" I asked, I wonder what her beautiful brain had decided she was gonna distract me with.

"Guess," she echoed. She smiled up at me, mischief laced her tone as she threw my own word back at me. She tugged at the buttons on my pants, opening them up – I leaned back allowing her more room to work with.

Her warm fingers pulled my cock out of my pants –it gently throbbing in her hands. I nearly held my breath waiting to see what she would do next. She looked at me as her grip tightened lightly on my cock. I kicked my pants off of my ankles and across the room.

I held her gaze as my breath picked up. Her tongue darted out running over her lips, before disappearing into her mouth. Barely parting her lips, drool started to seep from between them, over her bottom lip and down her chin. I watched as her drool slowly dripped down her chin, and then off of her chin, hitting the floor. She lent forward, a warm drop of her saliva hitting the tip of my cock. I jerked slightly as it hit my sensitive skin. *Damn that was hot.*

Slowly she kept leaning forward, more of her drool sliding down my cock. I fought my every muscle to keep still and let her do what she wanted. The tension in my body heightened the pleasure her touch gave me. The smallest movement in her touch sent waves of pleasure over me. Slow her drool made its way down my cock, sliding to my balls, some dripping to the floor, some continuing down my thighs. Her gripped tighten on my cock, briefly, as she stared down the head of my cock. Time stilled as she took me in with her eyes –slowly she blinked once before bowing her head towards me. Her lips gently grazed the tip of my cock. *Oh Goddess!* "Sage," I groaned, flexing my hand to avoid grabbing at her hair. "Good?" She pulled her lips off of me, looking up, a grin gracing her gleaming lips.

"Yes," I groaned. I bucked my hips slightly, grazing the head of my cock against her lips. Sage stuck out her tongue, sliding it over my head. A groan left my lips, I tipped my head back till her tongue left my skin.

Her lips meet my cock again, this time not stopping at my tip. Slowly sliding down my shaft taking me into her soft mouth. The wet warmth of her mouth seeped into me, warming my flesh. Gentle, once a good portion of my cock sat in her mouth, she sucked in, pulling another moan of pleasure from me.

Her mouth made beautiful sucking sounds as she fought to take more of my cock in her mouth. Saliva bubbled out from between her lips, the coolness of her saliva contrasting with her hot mouth. I had a river of her saliva running down my thighs in only minutes.

My heart beat pounded in my cock throbbing dangerously, bucking up against the roof of her mouth. Her strong tongue worked around my shaft, keeping me in her mouth. I looked down at Sage, she was looking back up at me, a loud groan leaving my lips. Her stunning mouth teased moan after moan from my lips, I reached over my hands sliding gently in her hair. Silky strands of her hair curled around my fingertips as I rushed to grab on to her.

"Sage," I moaned, her only answer was a strong tug as she sucked my cock deeper into her throat. A damn broke in me, pleasure riding my body in waves, as I orgasmed deep in her throat. Cum filled Sage's mouth, a small amount sliding down her chin, the majority of my seed had stayed in her mouth. My pleasure soaked brain took in the sight of her swallowing the last of my load that was in her mouth.

Oh Goddess! I slumped against the counter, catching my breath.

Sage

The last couple hours have been a whirlwind of pleasure and pain. Kissing and cuddling broke up the rounds of serious talking. I wandered down the hall pack house, lost in my memories. A large shape shifted in front of me snapping me out of my daze. The large shape changed into a person.

"Luna," a man greeted. The man walked past me. *What?* I kept my head down, watching where I was going. I passed a couple more people on my way to Nox's office, each nodding or waving at me as we passed. *Who are these people?* "Morning,"someone greeted.

"...Morning..." I stumble over my greeting.

"Luna!" Jake came jogging up to me, at least someone I recognized. "How are you?" he asked.

"Good. Yourself?" I asked.

"I'm ok. You look good." We lapsed into awkward silence as we stood in a random hallway. "Where are you going?" he asked.

"Nox," I answer. The air was starting to get warm, my clothes touching my skin, rubbing in all the wrong places. I glanced round at the walls. *Were they always this close?* "Me too. Shall we walk together?' he asked and I nodded and Jake starts walking, letting me follow him in silence. Jake enters before me, waving his hands around in a flourishing sweep. I snuck in around him, darting to the far corner. Nox didn't even look up at Jake, keeping his focus on the many maps spread out before him.

Nox looked up from his desk, his eyes settling on my eyes, after sweeping up my body. Satisfied that I was safe and well he returned to his task.

"We have a major problem. The pack is in unavoidable danger," Nox announced. Jake whipped around to look at me at Nox's words, as Nox up until now has kept me well and truly out of pack inner workings. *This is too much. I thought I could do this. This is too much.* My pulse raced, matching my breathing increase. " Started without me?" The room slowly filled with people I didn't know all adding their opinion into the mix. I backed farther and farther into the corner as the room filled.

"Move," Nox snapped loudly at the person standing in front of me, obscuring his view of me. "What?" The large man in front of me stood his ground. "Move! Now!" Nox yelled as he stood up, leaning forward, the malice in his voice palpable in the air. Several men standing nearer to Nox stepped back, folding in on themselves. The power rolled off of the two men, sparking in the air. "What is the issue with where I'm standing?" The power rolled off of him, challenging Nox. *Over where he is standing?*

"Move," Nox growled at him. He shifted to his left, slowly till I could once again see Nox. Nox sat back down, returning to the conversation at hand. "I want an answer!" the man yelled at Nox.

"Look behind you," Jake whispered at him, the sharpness in his voice not missed. The man quickly turned around to face me glaring, he started to open his mouth turning his anger on me. "Mr Howin as much as I respect your position in the pack as the head of your family line, I do not appreciate your behaviour and if you can not conform it to a respectful standard you will be asked to leave," Nox spoke before the man before me could turn his anger on me. He stuttered a few moments before turning back to Nox.

"Alpha," Mr Howin said, bowing his head, moving to the other side of the room, at the back. "It has been decided," Nox announced after what seemed like hours of everyone in the room taking over each other.

"We will be evacuating the pack for safety. As our Sister Pack we will reach out to The Half Moon Alpha in advance. All children and elders will be required to leave. "We will leave in groups of five and no more, we will use the marsh land as our evacuation route," Nox said. Everyone had fallen silent as Nox laid out the plan.

"What is the age range?" someone asked.

"Under 16, and over 65," Nox answered without missing a beat. "Those ages 16-21 will be guides and protective detail for our evacuating members," Nox paused looking out over the room, his gaze meeting mine. *This means I get to stay.*

"We will limit one sick or injured per group to maintain safety per group," Nox continued.

"How will we deal with parents?" a man in the back asked.

"One parent will be accompanying the children, with only one being permitted to stay, to avoid unnecessary orphaning of our pack." *Oh Goddess, the fact we have to take that into account.* "It's settled, we wait for word from Half Moon." The room was silent, all the needed details were hammered out, and assignments confirmed. Everyone milled around for just a few moments before quietly filed out of the room.

"Sage," Nox sighed, reaching out a hand for me. I peeled myself from the wall making my way across the now empty room, except for Nox and Jake at the desk. "I'm staying," I announced before Nox could say anything else. "What? Sage!" Nox gripped my hand pulling me close to him. "I'm not a parent and I'm not a child. I am staying," I repeat.

"I can't have you stay," Nox seemed desperately sad. "Please," he pleaded.

"It's dangerous!" Nox begged.

"I know," I confirmed.

"You are going," Nox pushed.

"No." I leveled my gaze at him, not budging an inch. "That's final," I said standing my ground. Nox let out a loud sigh, wrapping his arms around me, I held my arms down at my side. "You didn't hug me…" Nox's voice cracked, sadness coating, dripping from his words. "Please," he begged. My heart cracked at the pain in his words. He pulled me closer, breathing in my scent. *Mate.* "Why?" I asked.

"You could get hurt," he whispered in my ear. I fought to keep eye contact with him, fighting the tension and the power. "I'll get hurt more if I leave," I reasoned. Nox signed, placing his head on mine, pressing his lips to my forehead.

"I belong here." I lifted my arms wrapping them around his waist. "You do," Nox conceded. *I love you.* I took a deep breath, his scent curling a gentle arm around my soul. "I love you," my voice stumbling over the syllables. "I love you too," he echoed.

"Promise?" I asked.

"Promise," he reassured.

Sage

The last three days were a panicked mess of packing. I was overwhelmed by the number of children who were in fact part of the pack. I worked hand in hand with the daycare, paired up each child with the parent that was joining them in Half Moon. Helping the children pick which items they were bringing. Encouraging them to choose one or two items they loved, and opting into more useful items. Spare shoes and clothes were handed out to each family. Parents and older siblings supplied food and water for the younger pack members.

Nox spent his days planning with the pack members staying behind how they were to fortify the land, what supplies were needed to stay here and what needed to be sent to Half Moon, to aid in their effort to temporarily absorb the majority of our pack.

~

The last group had left for Half Moon two days ago. Nox did not leave his office, shy of eating and showering, even opting to sleep in his office. Wolves run in and out of his office with reports, then left with updated orders. I sat quietly, with my arms around my legs, on the couch in his office. It was all too much, I had stopped eating.

"Cookie," Nox offered. Nox was standing above me, he looked exhausted, deep purple marring his under eyes. I looked at the cookie in his hand. "Yes." I reached out for the sweet treat, taking it from Nox. The smile on his face made up for the last several days. He sat down next to me, slumping into the couch, watching me eat the cookie. "Alpha!" A young wolf came hurtling down the hall, bouncing off the walls.

"They are here," the young wolf said. The cookie dropped from my hand to the floor. "Where?" Nox asked as he bolted up from the couch.

"East Woods near the cliffs." Nox ran out of his office, yelling orders as he went. I followed behind him as best I could, but each stride I fell behind. Nox was out of the pack house and in the courtyard, surrounded by hundreds of wolves. He was barking orders to every passing person. I waited watching the massive sea of people.

"We move out!" Nox ordered above the din of the crowd. *Wait. I'm coming!* Nox looked out over his people, he stopped when his eyes reached me. He stopped moving, looking at me. I stepped towards him, I jumped back as a group of men almost ran me over. Nox marched through the crowd over to me. Strong arms pulled me close, wrapping me against a warm chest. *Nox.*

"I can't keep up with you," I yelped.

"You aren't coming," he ordered.

"Yes. I am. We agreed," I snapped.

"I know," he said, softly.

"Ride on my back," he commanded. *What? He was not suggesting*
..

"You can't be serious??" I gasped.

"Entirely," he responded.

"People are gonna talk," I complain.

"Let them. And after this we will give them something else to
talk about with how loud you moan," Nox said, smirking. *Oh
Goddess. This man is too much.* "Let's go!" Nox shouted, before
shifting. Nox's wolf form impressed me every time I saw it.
Nox's eyes stared back at me. I ran my fingers through his
soft fur, along his face, down his neck, over his shoulders and
traced his spine. I took one glance around before swinging
my leg over his back.

The muscles tensed in his back as he shifted his weight, taking
a couple tentative steps, adjusting to my weight. Nox let out
one loud bark and took off running, the rest of the wolves
falling into line behind him.

I gripped his fur, leaning my body close to his as the wind rushed past my face. The landscape blurred as Nox ran towards the cliff, the gentle thud of hundreds of paws hitting the ground hugging me from all sides. Under five minutes and we were slowing down as we reached the cliff's edge. The dark green lush forest spread out in front of us, it cut off sharply half a mile from the bottom of the cliff. I slid off his back, glancing around at the wolves around me. Nox shifted back into this human form, every inch of him on show. Everyone taking his lead, following suit. Modesty a non-issue.

"Split in two. Unit A with me," Nox commanded as he waved his arm over his head, moving towards the path leading down the cliff. I watched half our group split off and follow him. It seemed forever before they made it to the bottom, fanning out along the ground at the base of the cliff.

I looked down at the forest, scanning for even the slightest movement. Nothing. Nothing. Noth.. a slight wind rustled the trees. A wolf shot out of the underbrush, then another and another, all stepping out without a whisper from the leaves around them. They matched our wolves, wolf for wolf, and then some.

So many more of them. One wolf shifted, walking forward from the group, Alpha Ron stood in the middle clearing. *Him.* Nox held up his hand halting everyone, he walked slowly up to meet him. I watched entrapped, the rest of the pack waiting at the top with me rustled with whispers.

Alpha Ron opened his arms walking towards Nox, an overly

large smile on his face. *No. NO. NOO. Not that smile.* As Nox and Alpha Ron came to a meeting point, the smile dropped from Alpha Ron's face. *NO.* The two Alphas circle round each other a couple times, testing each other.

"Challenge," Alpha Ron said, giving a mock bow. The horrific grin on his face had me pedaling backwards. No one moved, not even a gasp. "I challenge you, Nox." Alpha Ron left out Nox's title on purpose.

"One on One," Alpha Ron continued. The world stopped around me, going blurry around the edges, echoing sounds swirled and muffled around me. My heart thundered in my chest, pulsing through my whole body.

A strong hand caught my elbow as my knees started to shake, I glanced over at a gaunt Jake. A few voices float through my hazy brain. "What?" came from my left.

"No," on my right.

"Alpha. Alpha Nox," someone corrects in a growl.

"He didn't respect his title," a woman hissed.

"No," someone repeated.

"Alpha," a man called.

"I'll kill him," someone snarled.

"He will win," someone promised.

"Can he survive this?" a voice asked.

"Quite! That's his mate," someone hissed.

"What?" a man asked.

"His mate," a wolf hissed.

"Her?" a girl questioned.

"She's watching," someone noted.

"He has a mate?" a voice asked.

"She's so small," someone commented.

"She can't watch this," a voice begged.

"She shouldn't see this," another confirmed.

"I…" Nox started to say. I ran full tilt towards the edge of the cliff, the gasps and whispers of the crowd around me as I darted past them and right over the edge of the cliff with a massive leap. "Nox," I whisper.

"Shift child!" The voice whispered in my head. The ground didn't rush up to meet me like I expected, I gently fell head first towards the ground, I stretched out my hands to meet the ground.

Nox

The gasps and shouts from the cliff above me cut me off, as I turned to see what was happening. Sage had jumped head first off the cliff. She fell slowly, her clothes rippling around her, hair flying, glowing white steam drifting off her in large whisps. My world jerked as Alpha Ron connected with my unprotected side. Bone-y knuckles bouncing off my jaw, straining my neck on the impact.

I turned to face him, the growl started deep within me and rolled up. He backed up a couple steps, before launching at me again, this time his attack was with wolf teeth and not his fist. He shifted in mid-air. I jumped to the side, Ron hit the ground hard, spinning around all teeth and snarls. I shifted, baring my own teeth at him. We snapped at each other, claws, teeth and fur.

Each of us getting in a couple good nips, blood dripping from the both of us. *Sage.* I scrambled out from under Ron turning to the cliff. Sage was still falling in slow motion down the cliff, white smoke drifted off her hair, curling up into the air, wrapping around her body like many arms embracing her. The smoke trail behind her drifted together, forming the shape of a tail.

Her hands reached out in front of her, except they weren't hands but small white paws. She stopped falling, her white paws resting on nothing several feet off the ground, her hind legs setting down on a floor that wasn't there. A breeze that only seemed to affect the smoke floating around Sage picked up then died down. *She's stunning.*

Ron pounced on me, pinning me to the floor as I watched Sage. His warm breath panting on my neck. His teeth grazed the back of my neck. Sage's wolf tail flicked through the air as she seemed to walk down the air to the forest floor.

The build of her wolf was different, thinner, small and delicate. Her thin long legs are almost too small to support her. Blinding white fur, lay flat to her skin. Large pointed ears flicked around catching every sound. Her tail was too large for her body, a large fluffy white mass that seemed to float behind her, somewhere along the length it was more smoke then tail, petering off into little whisps.

Every pair of eyes were on Sage, all but one pair, Ron's. It was too late. I felt the sharp spike of pain as his teeth sank into my neck. Everything went dark, the last thing I was was Sage's snarling face disappear as Alpha Ron walked over my body towards her.

Then…

Nothing.

Sage

Nox's whimper broke my heart, before I knew what I was doing I was lunging forward. *He will PAY!!!* Ron met me head on, with a condescending growl. We each snapped out at each other, nipping at each other sides, legs and tails. Darting out of the way of each nip, lunging in for more. We circled each other in this dance for what felt like hours.

Ron slowed down watching me, his head lowered, teeth bared. A wicked grin pulled at his lips, showing off all his teeth. Ron snapped at me, darting forward to dodge his teeth. *No!* His teeth clamped down on my tail, it was a mere moment before he tugged pulling me backward. I torqued my body round to face him, pulling my tail from his mouth. Ron was gone when I got my legs behind me again.

My hips hit the ground before I realized I was hit, I was launched several metres along the ground, skidding to a stop. *I can't breathe!* A bone shaking howl erupted into the air, echoing over the trees for miles. *Nox.* Then before I could catch my breath, between one blink and the next… there was nothing.

~

The hum of life came first, with the blackness. *Where am I? What happened?* I fought my eyelids to open. A burst of pain hit my skull with the blinding light, I snapped my eyes shut. The groan I let out a strange sound to my ears.

I tried to pull my arm over my eyes to block even more light out, twisting to hide in the soft fabric under my head. "Sage?" A quiet croaked at me. *Nox.* "Nox," I garbled. A shadow blocked out the light. "What time is it?" I asked.

"One PM." *A whole day??*

"I lost a whole day?" I tried to sit up, and opened my eyes to look at him. A wave of dizziness hit me, followed by a wave of nausea. There was a potent silence as Nox didn't say anything for a time. "Sage," he sounded so small and sad. "Yes?" I held my hand over my eyes, fighting to open them. "It's been over a week." *A what? A week?*

"What?" I forced my eyes open, watering at the bright light. Nox's handsome face met mine, scrunched up in concern. His face was marred with a patch work of bruising, all yellow and green, several day old scabs criss-crossing his face.

"Nox." I reached out to touch his face.

Nox

It took most of the day for the doctor to clear her to return home. Sage curled up in my arms, in bed. I placed several kisses on her forehead, running my hands in slow circles on her back. *I don't ever want to stop this.* The hours slipped by so fast.

"Child." A familiar ghostly voice said. *Moon Goddess.* I looked up, there she stood in the middle of our room. Her hair was floating around her head creating a halo behind her. As she did last time I saw her, she floated several inches off of the floor, her feet flat as though she was standing on an invisible floor. "Child. I'm glad to see you in the world of the waking,"

"Her wolf," I cut in. The Moon Goddess stilled, unearthly still, turning to me, the smoke swirling in her eyes darkening. "She is a Spirit wolf." I looked back at Sage, her hair had changed, framing her face was a new white silver strand of hair hung in her face. "A what?" I asked.

"One of my hand picked spirit wolves." I waited for more of an explanation. She stood there in the eerie stillness. "The wolves I can not save from a dark life, I bless them with a Spirit wolf.

They will join me in the stars," she explained. *Spirit wolves?* "I have heard legends about them, stories for pups around campfires," I added.

"It has been a while since such gifts have been given," she hummed.

"What does this mean?" Sage asked, moving closer to the edge of the bed. "Take care of each other. I paired you for a reason." The Moon Goddess turned to face me before continuing. "Heal her scars, show her what love is," she affirmed. She then turned back to Sage. "Be his rock," she declared.

"Now sleep. You have a hard choice to make soon." She started to fade away. Sleep taking over my tired body.

~

I shifted groggy, warm light warming my chest, it filtered in softly through the window. I rolled over, Sage still asleep next to me. She looked so peaceful as the light lit up her face. I buried my nose in her hair, resting against her neck.

"Morning," I whispered. Sage blinked a couple times, her hands coming up and resting on my chest. *My sleepy girl.* "This is amazing," she grumbled. Her voice, half asleep, was music. I smiled at her, brushing her hair from her face. "Mate," she whispered, smiling back at me. "Yes. I am." I kissed her bare shoulder drinking in her scent. I watched her as she fought off her sleep. "I want to talk to you about something," I comment.

Sage looks up at me, some alertness back in her eyes.

"Ok. I'm all ears," she said.

"I have been planning your Luna ceremony," I admitted. I waited and watched how she reacted. Sage froze looking at me, she bit her lip, thinking, it etched all over face. "But.." she started to say. "You are my mate," I insisted. Sage nodded, biting at her bottom lip again.

"And I am the Alpha of my pack, you are my mate, you are the Luna of my pack," I lay out. I slowly laid it out for her. "If they don't accept me…" she started.

"They already know you are my Luna. It's just a formality," I reassured her.

"I don't know," she whispered.

"Please. For me?" I asked.

"You really want this?" Sage looked at me waiting. "I need your support," I explain.

"To be your rock?" she asked.

"…yes," I answered. *My rock.*

"Ok," she agreed.

~

The last two days were a bitter sweet chaos, planning Sage's Luna ceremony –many hours wrapped up in blankets together and sipping warm drinks discussing plans, what had to be part of the celebration, what could go, and what she wanted.

Sage kept shifting around, and rubbing her abdomen whenever she thought I wasn't looking. "What hurts?" I asked. I pulled the blanket up higher to cover her more. "What? Nothing hurts," she insisted. She refused to look up at me. "Please don't hide from me," I whispered,

"My hip hurts, and my lower back, and my knees. I feel a little dizzy, and like I'm gonna throw up. I'm cold too," she admitted, slowly, she let me into the pain she was feeling. *What was going on?* "Let's get you to a doctor." Sage started to protest, waving her hands at me. "Please," I begged.

"Ok," she agreed. Sage started to stand up, waving on her feet before her face went slack and she dropped to the floor in a pile. *SAGE!!!* I ran over to her pulling her into my arms, my whole world a blur, as my whole world sat unconscious in my arms. I scrambled around for my phone. "Send a doctor to my house now! It's Sage!" I'm not sure who I even called, just that I needed anyone who could send a doctor. I placed my hand on her forehead. *She's burning up!* I shifted her into my arms, taking the stairs two at a time. I needed to cool her down. She's burning up. *Cold bath.* She was completely limp in my arms.

The bath would not fill fast enough. I placed her in the tub letting it fill around her. *Where is the damn doctor.* I held her head, and neck keeping her supported. The water licked up her body, cooling her down finally. She started to shift, waking up slowly, shifting in my hands. "Sage," I begged.

"Nox," she mumbled.

"I'm so glad to hear your voice." A scent hit my nose, one I knew well these days, Sage's arousal. I looked down at her, lust swirling in her eyes. *Heat. She's in heat.* A clattering of footsteps sounded through the house as a doctor came crashing through the door. "Alpha," the doctor greeted, panting, standing wild eyed in the doorway.

"I'm sorry I panicked. I think she's in heat," I gushed at the doctor.

"Nox." Sage reached out to touch me. "Let me see." The doctor settled down beside me, taking her temp, asking questions, I just sat back and watched as she worked. Sage kept getting distracted by me, looking over at me and having to get the doctor to repeat what she had just said. "You are right. She is in heat," the doctor confirmed.

"I should have seen this coming," I mumbled.

"Couple more questions, these ones are for you," the doctor said.

"Ok."

"You mated?" I fought the embarrassment clawing up my

throat. "Yes," I answered.

"She's not marked?" they asked.

"Correct," I respond.

"How long has she been at the pack?" the doctor asked.

"Couple months," I guessed.

"How long has her eating and weight been better?" the doctor asked.

"A month or so," I guessed.

"What can I do for her?" I asked.

"Mark her. Finish your bond," the doctor replied.

"If she isn't ready for that?" I asked.

"She will be ok. She will be in some pain and feverish, that should only last a couple weeks," they mused. *Weeks!* "Weeks?" I bluster.

"Nox," Sage whispered, as her hand wrapped around my sleeve. "You have this from here," the doctor commented. The doctor left, leaving me with my suffering mate and no way to help. After an hour, I helped her from the tub, and to our bed. Now instead of a fever, she was freezing. "What did the doctor say?" Sage had buried herself in what felt like a hundred blankets.

"She said that you are ok, that it will be over in a couple weeks," I responded.

"That's all?" she asked.

"No," I mumbled. She waited looking at me from under her mountain of softness.

"She mentioned that it would help if we finished our mate bond," I responded.

"How?" she asked.

"Marking," I admitted. Sage went quiet, I know marking was too much for her. *I shouldn't have said anything.* "I'm not ready," she said.

"I know," I agreed. I reached over, pulling her close, breathing in her scent. *Oh Goddess she's so perfect. My rock.* "I'm tired," Sage whispered, closing her eyes. "Sleep." I kissed her head and settled down next to her, closing my eyes too.

~

Two days. TWO DAYS! She has been sleeping for two days. "Nox," she mumbled. *Oh thank the Goddess I missed that voice.* "Sage," replied. I smiled at her. "What's wrong?" she asked.

"Nothing," I lied.

"Don't lie to me, you have been crying," she gasped.

"I missed you," I confessed.

"I'm right here," she reassured.

"You were…" I couldn't say it. "You were asleep… for two days."

"Doctor says it's because of your heat," I added.

"Mark me," she blurted.

"It's ok we don't have to, you're not ready," I whispered.

"I am,"she confirmed.

"You sure?" I asked.

"Yes," she whispered.

"When?" I asked.

"Now!" she yelped.

Sage

I picked at the edge of the blanket one more time, fiddling with how we were in bed. "You sure?" Nox asked for the hundredth time in the last ten minutes. "Yes." I pulled myself out of the little nest I had made around us. Crawling over to Nox, wrapping my legs around him sliding into his lap. A small smile graced his lips as my weight settled into him.

Nox gently traced a finger down my neck, stopping where his mark would sit. "Sage," he whispered peppering small kisses behind my ear. His lips trailed down my neck to my shoulder, nipping at my skin lightly. "Ready?" *No.* "Yes." Nox's hands gently cradled me in his arms, his hands rested on my back. His breath fanned out over my skin, giving me goosebumps.

"Please," I whispered. His lips danced over my skin before his teeth sank into my skin, burning erupted all over my shoulder. My fingers reacted -digging into his skin, leaving little half moon cuts in his arm, and shoulder. He released my shoulder, and the rush of fresh air over my wound brought a harsh sting with it. Nox's tongue lashed out, licking at the wound –slowly the pain eased to a pleasant hum.

"How do you feel?" Nox kissed the sensitive puckered skin around his mark. "Good." I eyed his neck. *I'm not sure I can do this.* "You can do this,"I hummed. Nox cocked his head to the side, exposing his neck to me. I paused, filling my lungs, steeling my nerves. I ran my nose down Nox's neck, delighting in how his breath hitched. Instinct took over as my mouth reached the crook of his neck. My canines snapped out, sliding smoothly into his skin. My teeth throbbed with Nox heart beat. My hips rolled forward in Nox's lap, my upper thigh rubbing against his very hard dick.

Nox didn't make a sound, but his hands gripped me tighter. I pulled back, licking at his neck. The skin healing right before my eyes. *"Sage,"* Nox's voice echoed through my mind. I jumped looking at him. *I can't handle this.* Nox tucked my hair behind my ears, looking at me. Gently in my mind I reached out to the new tether linking our minds.

"I can't do this," I link.

"That's ok, we will stay out of the link till you are comfortable," Nox voiced. "Really?" I asked.

"Of course," Nox soothed.

"I love you," I whispered.

"I love you too Sage." I looked up at Nox, the swirling dizzy feeling was beginning to leave my body –the pain receding too. I reached out to slide my hands into his hair, tugging lightly smiling at him. "How do you feel?" He could just have reached out through the bond and felt how I was doing but he didn't. "Good," I replied. I leaned up against his chest.

"Sage?" he asked.

"Yes?" I questioned.

"You still smell delicious." He nipped at my shoulder playfully. My lips met his, and we quickly caught fire –our kiss turning to a passionate dancing of our tongues. Our hands roam over each other, pulling the last of our clothes off. "Sage," he said my name like a prayer. I gently pushed Nox down til he was sprawled out on the bed before me. His cock hard, and bouncing with anticipation –I could not pull my eyes off of him. I quickly climbed on top of him, hovering above him. Gently I eased myself on to his cock, having to pause frequently to adjust to his size. Nox kept still letting me work my way onto his cock.

After several minutes I was fully seated on Nox's hips –my full weight on him. I looked up Nox's body. Nox laid there the picture of relaxed arrogance, his arms resting under his head –a smirk painting his face. In his eyes lust danced like sweet spice, its partner, love swirling like dark ice.

"Sage," his voice silk that brushed against my mind. I leaned forward, rocking my hips, I wanted to wipe that smug smile from his lips – to hear the desperate pants as he was swept away in a tidal wave of pleasure he could not fight. As my hips sank back down this smile faltered slightly, his lips parting. I smiled in triumph, Nox's smile grew wider.

"You are good but I am better," Nox whispered in my mind. Now it was a battle of wills –and I would not lose. Nox reached out wrapping his hands around my hips, holding me in place. A wicked smile curled his lips as a gasp escaped me.

"One point for me." he bragged. *Game on.* Nox bucked underneath me, keeping my hips in place with his hands. I leaned over placing my hands on his chest to balance myself. Looking at Nox I bite my lip slowly, my tongue sliding over my bottom lip.

"Damn," Nox whispered. It took me a moment to focus on the muscles in my core, clenching them around Nox, a spike of pleasure rolling through me. Nox let out a little groan.

"One point for me," I threw Nox's words back at him. Nox shifted his legs behind me –the only warning I got before he flipped us over. My back bounced as I hit the bed, Nox gently pinned me into soft blankets.

It was a battle of pleasure –giving and receiving fighting to have the other succumb to the pleasure first. Neither of us broke. "Sage," Nox growled my name in my ear. I licked over his fresh mark, nipping at it lightly. "Sage," Nox moaned my name as the bond between us opened up, the waves of pleasure rolling through it -as Nox climaxed tipped me over the edge joining him.

Gently Nox tucked me up in his arms. We sat in bed, our bond wide open basking in the pleasure of each other. "Take this." Nox handed me a small flat piece of plastic and metal, a single pill sitting in the middle. "It's birth control since you are in heat." I took the pill tossing the packaging in the garbage settling back down in his arms.

"We should shower," Nox suggested some time later. "Do you want to shower first or should I?" I asked.

"I thought we could shower together," Nox suggested. *Together.* "Ok."

~

The water felt amazing on my skin, washing the sweat away. Nox filled his hands with some citrus scent soap, rubbing it in his hands to foam up the suds. Slowly he ran his hands over my skin, starting on my shoulders down my arms. Nox slowly, taking great care, washed every inch of me.

Nox quickly washed himself before rinsing us both off. Nox moved on to my hair, massaging my scalp with shampoo –then gently tipped my head back to wash it out. *This feels amazing.* "Can we do this more?" I asked.

"Everyday," Nox answered.

"I love you," I whispered.

"I love you too." Nox stepped out of the shower, grabbing

towels – he wrapped me up in a huge fluffy towel. A smaller towel was wrapped around my hair, Nox starting to massage the water out of it.

The day continued in a mist bubble of love.

Sage

My fingers dug into the ground, clawing at the dirt floor beneath me. The rattling of the chains around my wrists grating on my brain. I pulled at the rusty chains locked around my wrists. Every movement burned as the metal bit into my skin —blood running down to my elbows.

I was back. It all had not been real. I curled up resting my head on the floor. NO! I smacked my head against the floor and the spark of pain flared through my skull. I continued to smack my head again and again against the ground.

"Stop that racket!" Nox stood on the other side of the bars. I looked at him —it was Nox, looked like him, smelled like him but it was not my mate behind those eyes.

"Did you really think you were special? Did you really think anything would change? I got what I need from you." No! Nox looked at me one more time before turning and walking away. As he reached the corner of my cell he kicked over the pail that constituted my bathroom, the sewage spilling all over me. I gagged and retched at the smell —Nox disappearing with so much as a glance back.

"Sage!"

"Sage! Wake up!" My body jerked, startling me. Nox's worried eyes looked at me. I scrambled to get away from him. *"Sage,"* he whispered down our bond. The warmth and love that had been missing from his eyes was back. "It's not real. You were asleep. It's not real," Nox whispered, staying just where he was –in our bed.

"What happened?" he asked. I looked at him. *I can't...I..* I closed my eyes, reaching for the bond between us. Letting the memory of my nightmare filter through it. Nox grabbed my arm clinging to me, his eyes glazed over. He blinked away the haze in his eyes, tears sliding down his cheeks. "Sage. My mate," he whispered to himself.

Nox

I bundled up my nerves and tucked them away in the back of my mind –today was about Sage. After painstaking days of planning and setting up, that day had come –her Luna ceremony. The bundle of stress that was my mate sat on the floor in a ball. We could hear the sound of the crowd over the music. The whole pack was out there –in her support, not that she could care the difference. "Beautiful." I ran my hand over her head –her face tilted up looking at me with her big heart melting eyes.

"I'm ready." She stood up, ignoring my hand to help her, brushed herself off, turning to the stage. "They have waited a long time for this," I whispered as she peered out at the crowd. "And you are exactly who they need." Sage turned to me, playing her hands on my chest, bouncing up to her tiptoes to kiss me lightly before turning and walking out onto the stage. *I am the luckiest person of all time.*

Everyone was dead silent watching her as she walked out along the stage and stopped in the middle –right in front of the large black throne. The throne was a massive piece, made of twist iron – it was large and imposing and had sat every Alpha of this pack. I waited one more beat before stepping out to join her. I stood next to her, directly in front of the throne, foreshadowing that I will soon be sitting on it. Slowly I raised one arm in the air, waving at my people. A loud cheer rose from everyone, a massive wave of noise –that stopped when my arm dropped back down. *How does her ceremony give me more power?*

I step to the side extending my arm to show off Sage, not a single sound from the crowd. *This is where I sit and she bows at my feet. No that's not happening.* "Sage." I reached out through our bond. *"Nox,"* she replied.*"Trust me."* I reached over and took Sages hand gently in mine, I stepped back a couple paces, guiding her with me. Panic flared in her eyes at the change of plan. I paused as she now stood in front of the throne.

I stepped in front of her shielding her from the crown, opening up our bond slightly letting my love for her seep through. Slowly I guided her back till she was right over the throne, having to balance to not sit down on the throne. "Sit." I breathed down our bond. She looked at me, I could feel the thundering of her heart in my ears. I nodded, gently placing my hand on her shoulders, encouraging her to sit. Slowly she sank into the throne. *Oh Goddess she looks perfect, like it was made for her.*

I smiled at her before slowly sinking to one knee bowing before her. I kept going down to two knees, then bending down placing my forehead next to her feet. The eruption of sound that came from the crowd shook the ground –the cheers. I slowly stood up, once I reached my full height Sage stood up too –tears glistened in her eyes. Pride filled my chest as the pack had accepted my amazing mate as their Luna.

Sage and I took some time to be together before joining the pack. The formality had fallen away, platters of food and drinks circled through the room. I scooped up a couple drinks, passing one to Sage. She glowed with a warm pink light of happiness. As we weaved through the crowd people stopped and talked not just to me but to her as well.

Gently at the back of the room a band struck up, a light instrumental melody. The centre of the room started to spin as people started to dance. There was no rhyme or reason to the dancing. Each person moved to the music, swirling and twirling around each other, some in large sweeping motions, other with grand arm movements and some with exquisite balancing acts. Sage watched the dancing, sipping and nibbling on food and drinking the whole while.

"I have a surprise for you," I revealed. I gently pulled her from the room, into a back hallway. Once we were alone I started to pull my shirt off over my head. "You know I know what's under there. It's not a surprise, not that I don't like it," Sage giggled blushing.

"Smartass," I jested. I finished pulling my shirt off to reveal the fresh ink underneath. Immortalized in my skin was her curly writing – her name. Sage. Right over my heart. It was still pink and sore as it was only a day old. "I love it." She placed her hand next to it, feeling every beat of my heart, that only beat for her.

Sage

What am I even doing here? The last several weeks had been peaceful, but hard in another way. Meeting after meeting, paper work, after Alpha Ron attacked our pack crossing a line in the treaties set out by the Council of Elders all his horrific acts came to light. Old wounds opened, but this time they did not hurt so much. All leading to this evening. A huge room filled with all the leaders, Elders, Luna's and Alphas, everyone with an ounce of power, from what seemed like every pack in the world.

I picked at the tulle on my dress, it rubbed my skin, driving me up the wall, the corset like top half pinching in all the wrong places. Every inch of my skin crawled, everyone kept looking at me and whispering to the people around them.

Waiters came round all the tables placing plates of food in front of everyone, salmon, turkey, chicken, beef, tuna, soup, salad, roasts, pasta, every type of food you could think of.

I had picked a stunning avocado salad that looked amazing as it was placed in front of me. I could not slow down as I shoveled every bite into my mouth –just melting at the taste.

Nox chuckled slightly beside me. *"Enjoying your food?"* I had become a lot more comfortable with the bond in the past weeks, it allowed me the privacy to seek his comfort without interrupting the flow of work that needed to be done.

"I don't claim to be an expert on meetings, but this is nothing like what we have been doing lately," I mused to Nox, smiling carefully at the others sitting at our table. A couple of small snickers rose from a young Alpha across from us that Nox seemed to know well.

"It will start to feel like a meeting soon," Nox said smiling at the other Alpha, seemingly in on the joke. Desert soon followed, an absolute mountain of fruit salad and ice cream was placed in front of me. The mango sorbet melted over the fruit creating a delicious syrupy sauce.

At the head table, sat the Council of Elders, two dozen men and women all wrinkled and gray stared out at the room. The room silenced as the man in the middle stood up. "Thank you for joining us," he started, his voice booming out over the room.

"We have many items on the agenda to discuss this evening, so I will dive right in. In an atrocious set of events it came to light the disgraceful accessions breaking our fundamental rules. The peace we have between packs, that we have kept for half a millennium, overseen by the Council before you. A wolf twisted the minds of his whole pack to hide his actions. Ronald Pikkered unprovoked attacked another pack – that is the least of the allegations against this man." *The least?! He endangered my pack! My family!* "I do not make light of the danger and pain he put that pack through, but in light of our investigation a long standing pattern of astonishing behaviour, unbecoming of an Alpha." He paused as whispered echoed around the room, everyone turning in their chairs to look at me.

"For this we strip him of his title." *That can't be all they do!* "The investigation, we on the council uncovered evidence of events that no one should ever have to experience. I will take this time to warn you that I will now be listing the offenses, each one in its own right enough to justify action against him. On the pack land we found seven different underground infrastructures that were designed to imprison upwards of 100 people, furthermore there is evidence that there were in fact people imprisoned within them. Not only was there evidence that people were imprisoned, there is evidence of brutal torture, and rape." The man swallowed pausing before continuing.

"When we questioned the members of the pack, it became clear that this was no secret, this behaviour was not punished within the ranks of its members, they believed it was fitting punish-ment, and or the right of its male members to participate in. The majority members were brainwashed into servitude, they did not see the wrong that was in front of them. Not only were they taught that this was normal they were taught that the rules that govern us were wrong, that the word of their Alpha was more powerful than the council."

"For those who wish to look into the details of the events and evidence there is an extensive report that can be requested. It is the decision of the council that Ronald be sentenced to a Council run detention facility, and collared off from his wolf. The members of his pack will be cared for those requiring psychological help, cared for and rehabilitated. We have reached out to those here today to take in the members of this pack. To teach them what love is to be in a pack. The members of the pack that actively harmed those under their care who knew the wrongs they committed and did not care the harm they did will join Ronald in his punishment." The man sat down, the room silent, one could hear the squeak of his chair. The woman to his right stood up.

"One more matter of interest has arisen from these events. Many may only know of it through myth and fable passed down to our pups through story, but like many stories there is truth and meaning behind it. The Moon Goddess has in fact blessed us with one of her beloved Spirit Wolves. It has been many thousands of years since one has walked among us. For each guiding spirit wolf that runs with her among the stars starts here with us." The woman talked with her hands, flourishing around her as she talked. Her hands rested on her chest as she looked up at the ceiling. "Spirit wolves come to us through her blessing only when they are needed, they heal broken bonds within our community. There is no one role or agenda these wolves must adhere to. Just their lives to be lived like us all. We all must live in the light of the Moon." She sat down, this time whispered scattered around the room after her words.

Next the youngest member – though well into her sixties, of

the council stood up to address the room. "Please take this time to mingle and discuss the events of the evening. We are stronger together."

Everyone started to talk and stand up, once again milling around the room. Nox guided me to the edge of the room standing just behind me, looking over my shoulder. The young Alpha we shared our table with sauntered over. "Alpha Nox." He greeted Nox shaking his hand. "I must thank you," Nox responded, gripping the man's hand. "This is my Mate, Luna Sage," Nox introduced me. " A pleasure." The man smiled at me. "Sage, this is Alpha Rocke's, he is the Alpha of The Half Moon pack." *Half moon.*

"You took in our pack members for their safety," I confirmed.

"I did," he replied.

"Thank you."

"You, Luna, are most welcome." He smiled at me. Nox and Rockes talked for several more minutes before he turned to go. Many more Alpha's and family leaders, elders and more introduced themselves to us. *SO many faces, so many names, so many people.* My brain was starting to get foggy trying to take it all in. "Let's get out of here," Nox whispered to me, guiding me through the room before another person could stop us to talk."Why?" I dodged through the sea of people.

"Cause you look so good in periwinkle, I didn't know that was a colour before, but now it may be my favourite," Nox complimented. Nox was looking down at my dress. Once in the hallway, we picked up our pace, making our way through the maze of halls in this place. Nox paused at a door looking at the sign on the door.

"In here," he said pulling open the door. It was a single bathroom, all back tile and chrome. He closed the door behind us, locking it. "Stunning, but it would look better on the floor."

Epilogue

Nox tucked the loose strand of Sage's hair behind her ear. It was a habit he had picked up over the last year. Sage had never really learned how to tame her wild hair, and he loved her more for it. Though all her attention seemed to be on the movie she always had half her mind on the love she felt from and for her mate.

Nothing in her life had been easy, nor had the last year but it was a different kind of hard. The hard of healing and growing, the growth pains of learning to lead, and then learning to be a good leader. Life had slowed down, winter had fallen in full force and it wasn't until the last minute when snow was in the hair had they finished preparing the pack for winter.

This year she would not be cold, she would not be fighting to survive, she would be fighting to thrive, and though a fight it was a much different one. Sage had learned more about herself and the world she was now a part of.

Nox had learned what he had been missing and that a great leader could always do more, learn more, be more. He was more than a leader more than an Alpha; he was a partner, a mate. That the world did not sit on his shoulders. That sometimes protecting those around you meant letting them fight their own battles.

Nothing was perfect – but they were safe, for now. Settled in a mountain of blankets, watching a movie about a girl with two dragons at a war collage. "Farewell for now my child."

Bonus Chapter

Summer

Sage

We sat in bright blue plastic chairs across from the doctor. She was a thin older woman who seemed very sharp but when she opened her mouth she was kind and soft. Nox had explained that she was a doctor just for the woman in the pack. She was a specialist in fertility, obstetrics and gynecology. Which seemed impressive. Nox and I had been discussing having pups. Not yet but we were talking about our future - and with everything we went through this year together. Nox wanted me to see the doctor to see if my past would have any impact on my health. While I had been cleared by the regular doctors on my health.

"So tell me about your concerns," the doctor smiled at me. "We.." No starts but the doctor hold up her hand to stop him. "Alpha," she said letting an edge of respect and authority lace her tone. "I am asking Sage, her health, her body her voice," she said looking at Nox in his eyes. She then turned back to me waiting her hands crossed on her desk. "We are working

237

on planning our future," I stared looking at Nox who just leans back and smiles at me. "And with my medical history I want to know where I stand with my fertility," I stumble over my words a little.

"That is excellent . So I can running a couple test and we can discuss where you stand," she smiled at us. I smiled back at her. " I will not lie, there are some aspects about your past medical history that does give me some red flags, but there are lots of options and that is only the worst case. Lets see what we are working with," she stood up guiding us down the hall from her office and into an exam room.

Several scans and blood tests later, we were sent home to wait on the results. Nox made a big fuse over asking them to speed up to process -to which the doctor told him it would take as long as it took. Doctors acting in their role as medical professionals could over rule the Alpha on an individual care level. Something Nox seemed to be struggling with when it came to my health.

It took a couple days before we heard back from the doctor to set up an appointment to go over the results. Several hours later we sat in the horrid plastic chairs - I made a mental note to look into upgrading the chairs. Which I could do now that I was Luna I had a say here over things. People not just listened to me because of Nox they listened to me because of who I was by myself.

"I will not beat around the bush; we do have obstacles to work around," she said pulling out several sheets of paper. She went through each test and the result and what it meant. The impact of what my body went through had left my fertility very low - and on top of that I had a lot of scaring so even if I was to conceive keeping it till term would be a low possibility as well. I left the office feeling numb, I wouldn't have children of my own. Even with medical intervention the possibility for me to carry a pup was next to nothing. My heart broke in my chest that Nox would never be a father -he would have been the best father a pup could have.

Not only would we miss the joy of pups -but the pack would suffer. An Alpha with no heir left the packs future venerable. I'm sure Nox's mother would blame me -holding me responsible. *Is she wrong?* "I'm so sorry," Nox wrapped me in his arms kissing my forehead softly. The tears started to tumble at his soft words.

"Do you still want to try?' he asked as we walked into our house the trip home a blur. I looked up at him, he had his own pain tucked behind a mask of acceptance and warmth -but the sadness and pain was there. *I could see it.* "I don't want all the medical intervention," I whispered quietly -hoping he wouldn't see this as me taking away the last of the little hope we had. "But I want us to do what we can to let it happen naturally," I offered with a smile. If we worked so hard to have a pup and we still couldn't or if we managed to conceive but I couldn't carry it to term it would brake me. *I don't either of us would survive that.*

Nox settled down on the couch pulling me close. "Ok, I like that," he said smiling at me. He understood me, he understood my choice.

Christmas Eve

Nox

I was excited last year we didn't get to celebrate Christmas at all. This year I was making it a big deal. I had spent hours decorating the pack house with blue and silver decorations, snowflakes where painted on to every window. For our house I went more traditional and decorated it in green and gold. I may have gone overboard with the trees. Placing two live ones in pots by the front door, one in the living room and a small one in our bedroom.

Was it too much? Probably, but I don't give a fuck. I had enjoyed years of Christmas's while she rotten in a cell. I would make every single one something to remember for her. It had felt like the best and worst year of my life. I had found my beautiful mate and I had watched her struggle and grow. Even though she deserved an easy life after everything she went through - she didn't get it. Between dealing with the getting Alpha on convicted, and then finding out she may never have pups the year had been a roller coaster.

The door opened as I put the last couple shinny red balls on the tree in the living room. Sage came stomping into our home, he hair filled with large snow flakes. Sage stopped in the living room, her eyes wide as she took in the room. "What?" she asked looking at me. "Merry Christmas!" I hopped down from the back of the couch and bounded over to her. Pulling her into my arms and taking a deep breath of her scent -this never gets old. Sage glowed now that she was physically healthy, a warm glow to her skin her eyes bright as they looked at me.

"I have to finish up your gift. Don't come into the bedroom," Sage whispered to me. "Okay," I kissed her forehead and let her go. She scuttled up the stairs smiling at me before she disappeared from sight. Sage hadn't said anything about getting me some Christmas gifts, yesterday we had spent the day making gifts for the pack and had agreed we weren't doing gifts for each other- not that I stuck to that. I had gotten her some gifts weeks ago. *Guess if I'm breaking our rule she can too.*

An hour later Sage came dancing down, a small box in her hand. She set it under the tree before practically vibrating over to me. She was happy and excited -the best gift I could ever receive. My beautiful mate happy and excited about the future we have. *Even after everything.*

It was late the sky dark, we had finished up eating -Sage had spent the afternoon baking a chocolate cake for tomorrow. Ever since the first time she had baked she had loved the chocolate cake making it for every occasion. While she did bake other treats weekly she always came back to the chocolate cake. I licked the chocolate from her fingers as she giggled at me. "I know its not Christmas yet, but will you open my gift" Sage asked shyly smiling at me. Tomorrow would be busy and filled with many people. I could give her this moment with just us. "Absolutely," I smiled as she ran from the room reappearing with the dark blue wrapped box. She thrust the box into my hands. She looked like she wanted to say something to me -but just bit her lip nervously. Slow in the dim glow of the kitchen I opened the gift my mate had gotten me. Just us in our small world -everyone else forgotten.

I slid the lid off of the small brown box. I frowned at the items in the box. On the top was a piece of paper, several items loose under it. I plucked the paper up and unfolded it, reading it slowly. One small line of the paper stuck out to me. **Test results: confirmed.** I dropped the paper to the ground looking at the small soft hat and the plastic pregnancy test sitting on it. "Is this real?" I asked my throat choked tears -I couldn't look up at her. "Yes, I got Dr Janik to double check just to make sure," she whispered softly. I dropped the box to the floor, scooping up my amazing mate in my arms. "This is just the beginning and we could lose it but.." Sage trailed off as my hand slid over her stomach, my hand resting lightly over where my child is growing in her uterus.

"What ever happens we will be a family always," I whisper cutting her off. "Don't tell anyone till we know … it we know it will be ok.." Sage mumbled through her tears.

Acknowledgments

To Rena, my childhood pup who I lost the same week I published Broken Moon Spirit thank you for all the sweet memories growing up. It took me a long time to get to the place where I could process the loss of you.

To my readers, thank you for taking a chance on my debut novel, thank you for giving this explicit werewolf romance a try.

To my husband, thank you for all the hours of our time together you gave up to make my dream come true. Thank you for believing in me and this story.

Thank you to Kate who re-lit the spark in me to pursue my creative dreams. Who inspired me to take more from life.

Thank you to my best friend Maja for loving me through all the stages of writing this book. Since the start of this book in Middle School.

About the Author

Nesi is a first time author dreaming of bringing the worlds running
rampant in her brain to life. When not writing Nesi spends her time reading
and hoarding books like a dragon. Enjoying life with her
husband, German Shepard puppy and two spoiled cats.